Dropped Dead

A Henry Walsh Mystery

Gregory Payette

8 Flags Publishing, Inc.

Also by Gregory Payette

Visit GregoryPayette.com for the complete catalog:

HENRY WALSH MYSTERIES

Dead at Third

The Last Ride

The Crystal Pelican

The Night the Music Died

Dead Men Don't Smile

Dead in the Creek

Dropped Dead

Dead Luck

A Shot in the Dark

JOE SHELDON SERIES

Play It Cool

Play It Again

Play It Down

U.S. MARSHAL CHARLIE HARLOW

Shake the Trees

Trackdown

JAKE HORN MYSTERIES

Murder at Morrissey Motel

STANDALONES

Biscayne Boogie

Tell Them I'm Dead

GREGORY PAYETTE

Drag the Man Down
Half Cocked
Danny Womack's .38

Sign up for the newsletter on my website:

GregoryPayette.com

Once or twice a month I'll send you updates and news. Plus, you'll be the first to hear about new releases with special prices. If you'd like to receive the Henry Walsh prequel (for free) use the sign-up form here:

GregoryPayette.com/crossroad

Chapter 1

I SAT OUTSIDE THE Baymeadow Hotel parking lot with binoculars and a cold cup of coffee from Kate's Café. Ted Parker, the husband of Lynn Parker, had checked in earlier in the day. But it was my belief that although Ted had checked in alone, he wasn't alone in his room.

I looked at my watch. Ten fifteen. Ted hadn't left the hotel. And I didn't see any females enter the building after him. Not any who were alone at least.

Lynn Parker had hired me to watch her husband and bring her proof he was cheating on her with another woman. Ted had told Lynn he was going to be out of town on business for the night. A road trip, he told her. Yet here he was, not ten minutes from their home in downtown Jacksonville.

I was getting antsy. And hungry.

I walked into the lobby of the hotel and eyed the attractive woman behind the desk. I gave her a nod when she looked up at me and smiled.

I grabbed a newspaper from a coffee table and sat down. Ted didn't know who I was—at least I didn't think he did—but I held the paper up, like they'd do in the movies, and peered over it.

It was a slow night in the hotel, to say the least. I thought about how the place was dead. But it was a Tuesday night, so what could I expect?

I glanced back at the woman behind the counter. She must've wondered if I was a guest. I'd catch her eye and she'd look away. Like we were playing some sort of a game.

But that's when I heard a crash that caused me to jump to my feet. A deafening scream came from the woman behind the desk. I followed her eyes toward the back of the lobby and through the windowed wall between the inside and the outdoor pool area, with blue and white lights reflecting off the water.

I moved toward the door and looked outside. Broken and mangled lounge chairs were upside down covering what looked to be a body, nearly naked, covered in only a white bathrobe. I stood at the door, my hands ready to push on the handle. I turned to the woman behind the desk and pushed open the door. "Call nine-one-one."

Outside, I moved closer to the body. It was a male, bloodied and broken. I reached for his wrist. No pulse.

I moved the chairs and glanced up above, along the building. Twelve stories with rows of windows—some dark, some with lights on inside—and a balcony with each.

The body had come from one of them. The sound of crashing waves could be heard from off in the distance.

I kneeled down, pulled the robe back from his face and covered the rest of him as best I could. A lump grew in my throat when I realized who it was.

Ted Parker was dead.

· · · · · ● · ● · · · ·

Emergency Medical Services had arrived within minutes along with a dozen officers from the sheriff's office and on-lookers from within the hotel. TV news media began to appear.

I stood off to the side, away from the body and the investigators standing over it. Witnesses were being questioned. I wondered where they came from, considering it was me and the woman behind the desk. Nobody was in the pool.

Some were in their rooms and heard the crash. A few were said to be out on their balconies. I thought about leaving before being questioned myself, especially since the law might find it odd I was one of the few in the hotel who wasn't actually a guest. And I didn't want to have to go into why I was there.

I knew it was only a matter of time, and sure enough Detective Mike Stone of the Jacksonville Sheriff's Office breathed his cigarette and coffee breath in my face.

"You going to tell me you just happened to be hanging out in a hotel lobby at ten o'clock at night when a man dropped ten stories?"

"How do you know it was ten," I said. I knew he didn't have that answer.

He pulled a cigarette from a pack in his pocket and stuck it in his mouth. He held it between his teeth—too white for a smoker, I thought—and held the lighter in his hand, his thumb on top. "You out here panhandling?" He lit his cigarette.

"Was that supposed to be funny?"

He kept his eyes on me for a moment, then turned to the body, still lying in the same spot, surrounded by broken lounge chairs. "Can you just do me a favor and tell me you don't know the victim?"

I hesitated to answer any of his questions, turning back to look at the woman who was behind the desk, now standing in the middle of the lobby talking to a couple of deputies.

"I'll tell you what you'd like. But I was here when it happened. I was hired to follow him."

He took a deep drag from the cigarette, his forefinger wrapped around it as if he'd watched the tough guys smoke on TV and practiced it at home. "You know him?"

"I was hired by his wife," I said. "He told her he was out of town, came here instead."

"You mean, he's got a girlfriend?"

"I don't know. That's why I was here."

"But you didn't talk to him, before he jumped?"

I shook my head. "No, it's called undercover for a reason." I looked away, my eyes on the girl at the desk again, still trying to gain some composure. "What makes you so sure he jumped."

Mike dropped his cigarette on the concrete, stepped on it with his foot, and bent down to pick it up. He spit on his finger, tapped the end where the ash had been and tossed it into a can near the doorway. "Witnesses saw it."

"Saw him *jump*?" I looked up at the building. "All that concrete around the sides of the balcony. Can't imagine anyone here really knows if he jumped."

5

Mike looked at my chest. "Where's your badge?"

"My *badge*?"

He stared back at me. "That's my point." He started to walk away. "You don't have a badge. So stay out of this, Henry."

I walked back into the lobby and pulled my phone from my pocket. I called Alex, my partner at Walsh Investigations. Alex was the brains behind the operation. Maybe even the brawn, too, if I were being honest with myself.

Although my name was on the door, she liked to take charge. The only reason her name wasn't on the door was that's how she wanted it.

"How'd you make out? You see the woman I sent you?"

"What woman?"

"In the text."

I looked down at my phone, put it back up to my ear. "Oh, I missed it. When did you send this?"

"Half hour ago," she said.

"You called too?"

"Yes, a couple of times."

I waited a moment, turned, and looked back through the lobby, the place busy now that there was a little action.

I said, "Ted Parker's dead."

"Dead?"

"Yes. Dead. Very dead. He landed on top of a row of lounge chairs out by the pool."

I could hear music coming through the phone. "Are you having a party?"

"What? No..."

The music was gone.

"So what happened?" she said.

I walked back through the lobby, the yellow police tape across the door now, on the inside. "I'm looking at him right now. Poor guy had nothing on but the hotel robe when he hit the ground."

"What'd Mike say?"

"Said he jumped, but..."

"Suicide?"

"His body's twenty feet from the edge of the pool." I leaned over the police tape, my face against the glass. I said, "Well, I don't think he was making a dive."

"You said 'but.'"

"But?"

"You said, 'He jumped, but...'"

"Oh. I was saying, I don't know how anybody can say for sure what happened."

Alex said, "Why not?"

"The balconies are fairly private," I said. "Concrete walls on three sides. It's impossible to see what anybody's doing. I'm just saying, wouldn't surprise me they wrap it up, call it a suicide, and hit the coffee shop."

Alex was quiet for a moment. "You gotta give him a little more credit."

"Really? I asked why he thought it was suicide; he told me to mind my own business. If *I'd* said I thought it was suicide, he'd have a full-blown murder investigation out there."

I thought I heard Alex let out a little snort. Maybe not.

"You look at that photo?"

"Oh, right. Hang on." I looked at my phone and clicked on the text Alex had sent me. The photo was of an attractive woman, nicely dressed, standing next to Ted. I put the phone back up to my ear. "Who is she?"

"I thought maybe you would've seen her tonight. That's why I sent it earlier. When he was still alive."

I looked at the photo again. She looked like a model, although on the older side. "Where's this photo from?"

"An event Ted's company was involved with. Charity event, for the children's hospital."

"But why's she with him?"

"I don't know. I found them online, on the Facebook page."

"Lynn in any of them?"

"No."

"Does she have a name?"

"Olivia Peckham."

One of the deputies gestured for me to back away from the windows, and shooed me toward the front of the lobby, away from the scene.

"I didn't see anybody at all tonight," I said. "Hard to tell. I was here when he checked in, and nobody came in after. Some couples, a couple of other men. No women at all, other than one I wouldn't expect anyone to have an affair with."

I walked out the front of the hotel again. "I wish I could go up in the room. They're crawling all over the place now. Won't even let anyone on the elevator. I'll call you back."

Outside, I looked past the EMS vehicles, a fire engine, and six cruisers from the sheriff's office. Various uniformed men and women coming and going.

I walked along the sidewalk in front of the building on my way to the parking garage off to the side. A Mercedes with a woman behind the wheel drove out of the garage and onto the street. I pulled out my phone and looked at the photo Alex had sent me. I didn't get a good enough look at the driver, and when I took my eyes off the photo, the car was gone.

I called Alex. She answered on the first ring.

"I could be wrong," I said, "but I'm pretty sure I just saw the woman from the photo."

Chapter 2

I WAS AT MY desk when Lynn Parker returned my call.

Her voice was quiet and soft. "Why would Ted take his own life like that? I... I always thought he was too intelligent to do such a thing."

I looked up and watched Alex walk in the door with a to-go coffee in her hand. She walked toward me and placed the cup down in front of me. I gave her a nod and mouthed "Thank you," then said into the phone, "Lynn, I don't know how much this helps. But I believe Ted was alone in his room. I'd been there for a few hours and..."

"No, it doesn't matter right now," she said. "Ted's dead." Lynn cried on the other end.

"I'm so sorry about what happened," I said. I looked over at Alex with a cup of tea in her hand, seated behind her desk watching me.

"I'm sorry," Lynn said. "It's just so upsetting when something comes to such an abrupt end. Even though we had a rocky marriage for a lot of years, it wasn't always bad. At least before he became so distant, and became a man I'm not sure I knew anymore."

"I was thinking I'd come by," I said. "I can at least share everything I know."

"You mean you'd like to get paid for your time?"

I hesitated a moment before I answered. "Maybe it's not the right time for you, but I don't believe there's enough evidence to say he was having an affair." I sipped my coffee. "You can just let me know when it's a good time for us to get together. I'm sure you'll want more time before we—"

"How about you just send me what I owe you. There's really no need to wait any longer."

"Whatever you're comfortable with."

She was quiet on the other end.

"Listen," I said. "I don't know how much the officers from the sheriff's office shared with you, but..."

"To be honest, I was quite upset when they were here. Or at least in shock. I didn't really ask the officer, who was here, many questions."

I glanced over at Alex, hesitant to even bring up what was on my mind. "Lynn, do you truly believe Ted would have jumped from that balcony?"

"Are you asking if I think it was something accidental? Or... perhaps criminal?"

She didn't respond. "I think I'd like to just move on from here, Henry. I hope you understand."

I held my tongue for a moment, of course surprised by her cold response. "Okay, I understand. I'll process the invoice and bring it over tomorrow."

"That sounds good to me, Henry. And thank you for trying."

She hung up, and I sat still for a moment, caught up in my own thoughts. Her words stayed in my head. "Thank you for trying."

Alex had her eyes on me. "What'd she say?"

"She thanked me for trying. And hung up."

"That's all she said? Thank you for trying?"

I picked up my coffee and held it in front of me before I took a sip. "She cried for a few seconds, but not much else. Showed little emotion. Didn't seem to care in the least."

"About his death?"

I nodded, then finally sipped my coffee.

Alex stood up from her desk. "Maybe she's dealing with it in her own way. Everyone handles these things differently."

I sat and thought about it all, from the first time she called until now. I had questions, to say the least.

"What was her response when you mentioned the possibility it may not've been suicide?"

I shrugged. "She just wants to move on."

"Oh."

"She was an odd client from the beginning," I said. "Like she never really believed he was cheating, but maybe just hoped to catch him."

"It couldn't have been about money," Alex said. "She has plenty of her own."

I stood from my desk, walked over to the window, and stared out at the St. Johns River.

· · · · •· •· · · ·

Alex and I were at the bar at Billy's Place, my friend's restaurant downstairs from our office. In fact, Billy wasn't just a friend. He was also our landlord. We had a nice office overlooking the St. Johns River he built for us over his restaurant. And the best part was it was less than a mile from the marina where I lived on a boat.

Billy was behind the bar as he always was. He put a beer in front of Alex and poured a shot of Jack Daniels and dropped in two ice cubes. He slid the glass in front of me and leaned down with his hands on the bar. "How's your client handling the news?"

"I was glad I didn't have to tell her myself. A couple of officers went to see her first. So she'd already gone through the shock." I shrugged, held my glass of Jack in front of me. "It was hard to tell how she's handling it."

Billy pulled a towel from his shoulder and wiped his hands. "Can't imagine what it's like having to hear your husband jumped from a hotel balcony."

Alex looked up at Billy. "I wasn't on the call with her, but it sounded like she's doing better than you'd expect." She gave me a quick glance.

Billy cracked a slight smile and leaned over to wipe the space on the bar next to me. "Maybe she did it?" He laughed and walked away, toward the other end of the bar.

Alex turned to me. "Don't even think about it."

"About what?"

"Don't start overthinking this. Let's just leave it up to the sheriff's office, okay? We did what we were supposed to for our client. So let's just get paid and move on, the same way Lynn Parker would like to." She kept her eyes on me and sipped from her bottle. "And maybe we can once again agree not to take any more cases with cheating spouses."

I looked up at the TV on the back of the bar, although I couldn't even tell you what was on. My mind was already shifted into gear. I turned to Alex. "Don't you think we should at least see who the woman is from the photos?"

Alex paused, then shook her head. "No. But how about this? I can tell Mike... and, like I said, we'll let the sheriff's office handle it from here."

I watched Billy talking with some customers down the other end of the bar.

A well-dressed gentleman in a suit, but without a tie, stood and watched him. The man leaned forward and said something to Billy, but I couldn't hear a word. I thought maybe he'd just ordered a drink.

Both Billy and the man turned and looked down the bar toward me and Alex.

The man walked alongside the bar and stopped at the empty stool next to me. "Henry Walsh?" he said.

I put my glass down and looked at him. "Do I know you?"

He kept his eyes on me for a moment, glanced at Alex, then shifted his gaze back to me. "My name is Jack Parker."

I straightened myself up in my seat. "Jack Parker?" I made the connection right away. "Are you Ted Parker's—"

"Yes." He nodded. "I'm Ted's older brother."

I glanced back at Alex, then stood and reached out my hand. "I'm sorry about your brother."

Jack shook my hand and nodded.

"This is Alex Jepson," I said. "My partner."

He reached in front of me and shook her hand. "Nice to meet you," he said.

"So, is there something we can do for you?" I said.

He looked up. "I understand you were there the night Ted died?"

I felt a lump in my throat. But I tried not to swallow. "Who told you that?"

He shook his head. "That's not important." He glanced past me at Alex. "You were following him?"

I hesitated to answer. "If you can first tell me why you're here, I'll—"

"My brother was having trouble. I know his marriage wasn't great, which I understand is why you were there, and I'm not exactly sure his business was doing as well as he'd hoped. I don't know if he was depressed or not, but, I'm just afraid he might've been into something over his head."

Alex and I both watched Jack Parker, waiting.

He gestured toward the seat next to me. "May I?"

I nodded. "Of course."

Jack sat down on the stool as Billy walked over and asked him if he wanted a drink.

"Dewar's and soda, please." He pointed toward me and Alex. "And whatever Henry and Alex would like."

I sipped my drink. "So are you going to tell me how you knew I was watching your brother?"

"Actually, yes. I had somebody following Ted."

I said, "Someone who was there at the hotel? When I was there?"

"This person's a she. And, yes, she was there. But I haven't heard from her since that night."

"Why not?"

Billy put the glass down in front of him, and Jack took a sip, then shrugged. "I wish I knew. She hasn't returned my calls."

I sat back with my arms folded.

Jack said, "Is it true? That Lynn hired you?"

I wasn't sure how much I should share or what I needed to tell him before he told me exactly why he showed up looking for me in the first place. I reached for my glass and took a sip. "I can't talk about my client's business with someone I don't even know. And you haven't exactly told me why you came here looking for me." I finished my first drink and reached for the one Jack had ordered for me.

"I just wanted to make sure I had the story straight... that Lynn had really hired you. I just... I find it a little, I don't know, suspicious, I guess? That a private investigator she hired just happened to be there when my brother jumped to his death?"

I glanced at Alex, then turned back to Jack and straightened out on the stool. "Are you implying I might've had something to do with what happened?"

Jack held his gaze on me, then shifted his eyes to his glass. He shook his head. "No. No, I'm not. I just wanted to be sure. I mean, I wanted to confirm why you were there." He kept his eyes down. I saw a tear come down his cheek. "I miss him. I... I just wish there was something more I could have done."

Chapter 3

LYNN PARKER STOOD OUTSIDE in her driveway when Alex and I pulled up and parked a few feet from a stack of at least a dozen cardboard boxes and overstuffed garbage bags. Lynn was dressed in jeans and a long white T-shirt that looked like it belonged to a man.

We stepped out from the Jeep.

"What's all this?" I said.

She removed a pair of work gloves from her hands and pushed her hair from her face. "I'm not one for holding on to material things just for the sake of memories."

Alex stepped toward Lynn and put her hand on her back. "Are you doing all right?"

Lynn held her hands out wide and looked along the boxes and bags in the driveway. "I'm told this is the first step." She shrugged. "I thought I'd take care of it now; get rid of some of his things before I changed my mind."

It'd only been a day since Ted's funeral, and Lynn appeared to be moving forward, just as she'd suggested she'd wanted to.

I turned and walked back to my Jeep, leaned in, and grabbed an envelope from the glove box. I walked over and handed it to Lynn. "I didn't bill you for the final night."

She looked down at the envelope but didn't look inside. "Why not?"

"We just thought, well..."

"I didn't ask you to do me any favors, Henry. I appreciate what you did." She turned and started inside. "Tell me what the additional amount should be... I'll write you a check." She stopped at the door and waved for us to follow. "Come on inside."

We followed her in and down the hall toward the back of the house. She turned into a room, set up like an office, on the left, just before the kitchen. Alex and I waited outside the door and looked in at Lynn seated behind the desk. She pulled a checkbook from the middle drawer and opened the envelope. She removed the invoice and flattened it out, picked up a pair of reading glasses from the desk and slipped them over her eyes. She looked toward me and Alex in the doorway. "I'll add an extra two thousand to this."

"Two thousand? But our daily fee is only—"

"It's only fair, Henry. I don't understand why you're supposed to take less because Ted threw himself off the balcony. If he hadn't, you'd probably have at least another few weeks on your plate. Am I right?" She leaned her head down over the check and finished writing it out. She tore it from the leather case and stood from the desk, walked to the doorway, and handed it to me.

Alex and I turned and started down the hall toward the front door.

"I assume you've been in touch with the sheriff's office?" I said.

We stopped at the front door.

"No. Am I supposed to be?" she said.

Alex said, "Just that they confirmed it was suicide. Or at least didn't find any evidence of foul play."

"Oh," Lynn said. "As far as I know they haven't made it official... or whatever the word is. I guess that means it's still an open case?"

Alex nodded. "It shouldn't be long, from what a friend of mine over there told me. Maybe another day or two."

Lynn held her hand on the doorknob and smiled, tight-lipped.

I stopped before I walked outside. "I'm just curious," I said. Will there be any issues with his life insurance policy, because of the suicide?"

She shifted her eyes to the floor for a moment. "No, not because of the suicide. But, come to find out Ted had made some changes to his policy a couple of months ago. So I may have some things I'll need to deal with." She shrugged. "It's nothing I'm worried about right now. It was a small policy Ted had through the business."

Alex and I stepped outside and turned to her from the driveway. "But what do you mean he made changes? Why wouldn't you know about it?" I said.

Lynn stared down at me from the doorway. "I really can't answer that," she said. "And, clearly, neither can Ted. But I have a feeling he'd been planning this—or thinking about it—for quite some time."

"What were the changes?" Alex said.

"He decreased the amount. He actually cut it in half, to lower the premium." She sighed and stepped out into the driveway. "I appreciate you coming by. But I have to get back to my cleaning." She slipped the gloves back on her hands.

"One other thing," I said. "Ted's brother came by to see us."

"Jack?"

"Does he have another brother?" I said.

Lynn shook her head. "No. Just Jack. But what did he want?"

"He just wanted to get our take on what happened," I said.

"How did he know who you were?" Lynn said.

I didn't tell her about this so-called private investigator he'd hired to watch his brother. I wasn't even sure it was true.

Lynn kept her eyes on me for a moment. "Jack's got one of those minds... always thinks there's more to a story than what everyone else can see. He's one of those people, has trouble seeing the forest for the trees."

I stared back at her for a moment, and she turned, looked back into her house. "Do you know anything about Ted being in some kind of trouble with the business?"

She looked down at the boxes and bags in the driveway. "Ted was a complicated man. He was a thinker... and I guess he just couldn't take his own thoughts any longer." She looked up at me. "Thank you again. If I know anyone else who needs a private investigator, I'll make sure they call you." She turned to her steps and pulled open the door. She walked inside and closed it behind her.

We took 90 East toward the beaches and turned north on First Street. I looked to my right toward Jacksonville Beach. I thought about how much I wouldn't mind a break, kick back in the sand for a day or two. The truth was, we'd had a lot of lulls in our business. But it was hard to relax when you didn't know where your next check would be coming from. And I found myself being pulled deeper into investigating Ted Parker's death. Even if it meant it wasn't something that would put more money into the bank account.

The truth was, Alex and I had gone back and forth on where we wanted the business to go. Some of the work we'd taken was for local defense attorneys. So a lot of our days were spent going up against the sheriff's office. We'd built our reputation, and both Alex and I had gotten known for going above and beyond to ensure we'd find the truth. Sometimes that meant going on our own, without a client.

We couldn't help it.

I parked just outside the front of the Baymeadow Hotel and walked through the revolving door. I wondered if the same woman who was behind the desk when Ted fell from that balcony would still be there. It wouldn't have surprised me if she'd at least taken some time off after witnessing such a gruesome scene.

But sure enough she was there, helping an older couple with such pale skin I knew they were down from the north. She glanced over at me, but I couldn't tell if she remembered who I was. With a slight smile my way, she turned back to the couple and pointed them toward the elevator. She gave me a smile. "May I help you?"

Alex and I stepped forward.

"I don't know if you remember me," I said. "But I'm sure you remember the night I was here."

The smile disappeared from her face, and she closed her eyes for a moment. "I thought that was you."

"I'm sorry you had to witness such a tragedy."

A perplexed look took over her face. "Wait... were you even a guest here?"

I shook my head. "No." I handed her my card, then turned to Alex. "This is my partner, Alex Jepson."

She gave Alex a quick glance, then looked down at the card in her hand. "Private investigator? Is that why you were here that night?"

I nodded, but didn't go into details. I looked at the plastic name tag on her chest. "Ava?" I pulled my phone from my pocket and turned the screen toward her. "Do you recognize this woman? I believe she was in this hotel the night of Mr. Parker's death."

She squinted and leaned closer to the phone. "I... I'm not sure. She looks familiar. But I can't say for sure. If you have a name, I can look her up in the system."

"I wish I did." stuck the phone back in my pocket. "And what about Ted Parker? Had he stayed here before that night?"

She stepped toward the computer and tapped on the keyboard. "I'd never noticed him before. But that doesn't mean he was never here." She squinted her eyes and looked at the computer screen. "Okay, yes. He stayed here before. Six different stays."

"Alone?"

She shrugged. "I wouldn't know. We don't ask for anyone else's name other than the person who books the room."

"I know that," I said. "But..."

"He always requested a king. But that probably doesn't tell you anything, either." She typed on the keyboard. "Oh, wow... interesting. He stayed in the same exact room each time, on the seventh floor."

I thought for a moment. "Would you mind checking to see if a woman named Olivia Peckham has ever stayed here?"

She tapped the keys. "Peckham? P-E-C-K-H-A-M?" She looked up from the screen and held her gaze on me until I answered.

"Yes," I said. "Peckham."

She typed again, then ran her finger over the screen. "She stayed here last week. For two nights."

27

"Was she here the night Ted Parker died?"

She looked down at the screen and shook her head. "She actually checked out that morning."

Chapter 4

JACK PARKER WALKED THROUGH the door and toward the table where Alex and I were already waiting for him. Not only was he dressed more casual than the first time we'd met, but also looked more like his brother, Ted.

"Sorry I'm late."

I looked at my watch. "You're right on time."

His arrival was, at most, a minute later than he'd promised.

Billy's bartender, Chloe, delivered our drinks and placed them down on the table. I looked up at Jack. "I ordered you a Dewar's."

Jack sat down across from me and Alex. He picked up his drink and took a sip. He watched Chloe walk away, then shifted his eyes back to the table. "So, how can I help?"

I paused a moment. "Can I ask you to be straight with me?"

He put his glass down on the table. "What's that supposed to mean?"

"Exactly what I said." I didn't go into it any more than that, glanced at Alex, and continued. "Why did you come see us the other day? I'm not sure if you were there to confirm your brother's death was a suicide, or if you feel there may be more to it."

Jack looked from me to Alex and again picked up his glass. "I just wanted to understand the reason behind you being at that hotel the night of Ted's death."

I pushed my glass aside and leaned forward on the table. "What's the deal with you and Lynn? I get the feeling the two of you don't get along very well."

Jack looked down into his drink. "Lynn rubs a lot of people the wrong way."

I thought for a moment. "Well, she's certainly a straight shooter," I said. "Which I can appreciate."

Jack lifted his glass to his mouth and held it below his chin "Ted would have a few drinks, loosen up, and say she was nothing but a cold bitch."

Jack paused a moment. "She changed... became a different person over the years. Things just got sour over time." He looked down into his glass. "As I guess can happen to any married couple."

"Anything behind it?" I said.

He looked up at me. "You mean, behind their relationship falling apart? Lynn was jealous, especially knowing Ted dealt with a lot of women at work. She didn't always like that. But just because he had female employees and clients, doesn't mean he was messing around on her." He sipped his Dewar's. "She liked it better when she had more control over him."

Alex leaned on the table. "Control?"

"Lynn comes from a lot of money. They tapped into daddy's bank account when she and Ted were first married, and he was trying to get his business off the ground. So she always made sure he knew she was the one supporting them. And then, when it appeared the business was heading in the right direction, well... I'm not sure she was as happy about it as you'd think."

Alex took a sip from her bottle of beer glanced at me from the corner of her eye.

"So what do you do for work?" I said.

"Me? I'm in sales."

I finished my drink and nodded toward Jack. "You want another drink?"

He looked into his glass, finished what was left, and placed it down next to mine. "Sure, why not."

"I thought you owned your own business," I said.

"I do. I'm self-employed. But that just means I have a lot of bosses." He turned and glanced toward the bar. "I represent a number of businesses as what you'd call an independent sales representative."

"Is that like one of those schemes? Where you have to get all your friends to sell under you, and they get three people, and..."

He laughed. "No, it's not like that at all. It's a real business."

"Pyramid schemes," I said. "I remember growing up, the guy next door to us sold insurance like that. But he didn't really sell the actual insurance, he just tried to recruit people, and he'd make money off of them."

Alex had a look on her face, like she felt it was time I closed my mouth. She turned to Jack. "You never worked for Ted, did you?"

He shook his head. "No. I mean, he'd bring it up once in a while, see if I was interested. But I'm happy with what I do. And he has other people in his business..." He stopped when Chloe brought three more drinks to our table.

"Thanks, Chloe," I said, before she turned and walked away. I pulled my glass in front of me and let it sit for a moment. "So, Jack, what can you tell me about your ex-wife Olivia's relationship with your brother?"

"Olivia and Ted?" He shrugged. "Why?"

"I'm just curious about their relationship. It was mostly business, is that right?"

He paused a moment and looked like he tried to hide a swallow. "She... Olivia works for a company that makes lab equipment. Ted's her client."

"So that's it?" I said.

Jack gave a slight tilt of his head, his eyes narrowed. "What exactly are you getting at?"

"I'm just asking. Remember what I said when we first sat down? I asked you to be straight with me."

He stared at me across the table. "She was one of the people who helped him get the business moving in the right direction. Really went out of her way... got her bosses on board and everything, so Ted would have the equipment and machines he needed." He sipped his Dewar's and leaned back in his chair. His eyes moved around the restaurant.

I said, "Olivia was at that Baymeadow Hotel. The same one Ted was at, although she'd checked out the morning before."

I could see it in Jack's eyes his mind was working through the scenarios of why she might be at that hotel. I said, "Can you tell me what kind of car she drives?"

Ted took a moment before he answered, like he was in his own little world for a moment. "What kind of car? Olivia?" He looked off, past me and Alex, then nodded. "Last I knew, she drove a Mercedes."

"A white one?"

"Yes." He leaned down on the table and looked into my eyes. "Did Lynn ask you to investigate Ted's death? Or are you just a curious person?"

I smiled and huffed out a slight laugh. "Let's just say she gave us a small bonus. So I felt somewhat obligated to do a little more digging while we had some downtime. I drove by the beach earlier and thought I'd like to stick my feet in the sand. But I'm not very good at relaxing anyway."

Jack sat quiet, slowly nodding his head but maybe at a loss for words. "So what would Olivia have to do with any of this? Just because she was at the same hotel?"

"I saw a white Mercedes leaving the hotel later that evening," I said. "And if she'd checked out that morning, then I'm not exactly sure why she'd still be there."

He shook his head. "Are you trying to say they were having an affair?" He laughed. "No way. No chance. Ted was a scientist. A nerd, really. But Olivia, well, she was a party girl. She lived for herself. She could get any man she wanted." He looked down at his glass. "I should've known from the beginning she wasn't the marrying type."

"I'm not saying she was there with Ted. Or maybe she was, but it doesn't mean it had anything to do with sex." I looked at Alex and she rolled her eyes, although I wasn't sure why. Maybe she didn't think I had to say it the way I did. "We still don't know for sure if it was Olivia."

I don't know if that was a lie or not, but I didn't want to lead Jack down the wrong road. At least in his own mind. Not until I had more answers.

"She lives east of Jax now, out in Crawford," he said. "Has clients all over the southeast, so she spends a lot of time in hotels instead of driving back and forth. And the way she drinks..." He shot back his Dewar's and wiped a drop from his lip. "She must've just stayed there for business. Maybe she had a meeting with Ted."

Jack seemed like he wanted to defend her.

"I can talk to her if you'd like," he said.

Both Alex and I shook our heads.

"No," I said. "Not right now. I was just asking questions. If I need anything else or have any other questions, I hope you'll be open to it?"

Jack nodded. "Yes, of course."

I leaned on the table. "And one more thing, Jack. You mentioned when we first met you felt the business was in trouble? What'd you mean by that?"

Jack paused for a moment. "I'm just speculating. Of course, trying to understand why my brother would take his own life. But the thing is, his company was growing. But I'm not sure they were making a lot of money." He looked around the restaurant and kept his voice low. "There were a number of companies that wanted to buy them out."

"Was he going to sell?" I said.

Jack shook his head. "I don't think so. I don't think he was interested in letting it go, just so they could cash in." He shrugged. "Ted didn't always care about the money."

"Is there any chance this could've had something to do with Ted's death?"

Jack paused. "I think Ted's partners blamed him for holding them back from making a lot of money."

Chapter 5

I PARKED ON EAST Bay and walked toward the patio outside Bravado's Restaurant. I had been surprised a month earlier when I got a call from my ex-wife, Annie. She'd gone out to California to launch her dream of being a screenwriter, but turned out she'd spent the last few years on a crime novel instead. And until I'd heard from her, I'd be lying if I said I thought of her at all since we split.

But out of the blue she called because she was coming to town.

She was already waiting for me at a table when I stepped over the chain along the sidewalk into the seating area outside the restaurant.

Annie stood and gave me a hug before we both sat down across from one another.

"Congratulations" I said.

She smiled. "Thanks for your input on the book. It goes to the publisher in the morning. If I had time, I'd ask you to read it."

"What I did read was good," I said. "I'd tell you if it wasn't."

She nodded and gave me one of her looks. "I know you would."

My phone rang. I ignored it at first but pulled it from my pocket to look at the screen. "Sorry," I said. "I gotta answer this."

She gave me a nod. "You can answer it. You're on the clock, aren't you?"

I rolled my eyes. "I'm never off it."

It was Alex.

"Where are you?" she said.

"Downtown."

"With Annie?"

I hesitated a moment, as if Alex would be bothered. But she was the one who pushed me to go meet her when I wasn't sure I wanted to. "Getting something to eat."

The line went silent for a moment.

"I got my hands on the video footage from the hotel," she said.

"How'd you do that?"

"It's not important. But what is important is either you fell asleep out there in the car watching the hotel... or you weren't paying attention. Because there were a few men who'd gone in and out that night."

"Of the hotel?"

"You didn't see them?"

"I might have. But I was there looking for the other woman. It wasn't a murder investigation at the time."

"Okay, well, maybe you should come by and see what I have?"

"What about the white Mercedes? Did you see one in the—"

"The only footage I have is the camera in and around the lobby. You can see in front of the elevator, but that's it."

"I'll call you a little later. If it's not too late I'll come by."

I hung up just as the waiter walked up to our table.

Annie ordered a glass of wine. "You want another Jack?" she said.

I looked down at my glass. I'd hardly made a dent. "I'm all right for now."

Annie leaned forward on the table. "Are you okay?"

I hesitated a moment. My mind was moving in too many directions. "It's just this case we're working on is... "

"The suicide at the hotel?"

I stared back at her. "I told you about that?"

She shook her head. "I saw you on TV. I just happened to catch the news while I was getting ready. You were outside, at the front of the hotel, with officers from the sheriff's office."

I thought for a moment. "I didn't even pay attention to the cameras. I saw them there but..." I finally took a sip of my Jack and looked off for a moment. My mind had gone back to the case.

"Did you know him?" she said.

"The guy who was killed?"

She nodded. "They said it was suicide. But I had a feeling there'd be more to the story since you were there." She sipped her drink. "So what's the story? Why were you there?"

"His wife was my client. She suspected he was cheating on her. At least that's what she told me."

"Ted was the man you were watching?"

I nodded. "The wife didn't seem too upset, either, although I don't get the feeling she had anything to do with it. She seems smart enough... wouldn't make sense to hire me to watch her husband if she was going to have him tossed off the balcony."

Annie kept her eyes on me. "So the sheriff's office got it wrong?"

I started to shake my head but stopped. I was the first to point the finger, but for some reason I'd find myself defending their work. "There's a lot of crime in Jacksonville. They're not going to get them all."

She cocked her head a bit. "Are you the great defender of the sheriff's office now?"

I sipped my Jack and gently placed the glass down on the table. "I can't look at it like it's me against them. It's never about that. It's about getting to the truth."

Annie gave me a slight smirk and nodded. "I'm sorry, I—"

"Oh, you don't have to be sorry. I just... I can't focus on proving someone wrong all the time. That's all I'm saying."

She picked up her glass and looked off for a moment, then down at her watch.

"Do you need to go?" I said.

She let out somewhat of a sigh. She pushed her glass aside and leaned with her elbows on the table, her eyes looking down at her hands.

"Is something wrong?" I said.

"I was thinking of staying around here for a little while."

I didn't respond right away. "Oh," was all I could get out of my mouth. It was okay seeing her, but I wasn't sure I was ready to have her around all the time if that's what she was hinting at.

"What about the West Coast?"

She shrugged. "I'll go back at some point." She turned and looked out toward the St. Johns River. "It's nice around here. I miss it." She shifted her eyes to mine but didn't say much else.

Maybe she'd hoped I'd say more... that I'd jump for joy when she indicated she might want to stick around.

But that wasn't the case. It was okay seeing her, but whatever we had when we were younger was long gone. At least as far as I was concerned.

Chapter 6

I WALKED THROUGH THE front entrance of the building where Ted Parker's company was located. I was there to meet Tucker Dennison, one of Ted's partners in the business who'd become the interim CEO after Ted's death.

I walked through the glass doors into the offices and spotted a man leaning over the reception desk, laughing and flirting with the pretty young woman seated behind it.

She looked past him and tried to get the smile off her face, look serious, and stared right at me. "May I help you?"

"I'm here to see Tucker Dennison."

The man between us straightened and turned to me. "Henry Walsh?" He was shorter than me by a good six inches, although the sleeves of his dress shirt stretched around his muscular arms. "Tucker Dennison," he said. He reached toward me and shook my hand with a strong grip I'd expected.

He nodded toward another glass door. "Come on back." He walked ahead of me and slid a key card through an access pad next to the door, then pulled it open when it clicked. He gestured for me to walk in ahead of him. But he walked past me and turned down the hall.

I looked into each small office, some empty but others occupied with quiet workers, their heads down at their computer screens. "How many employees do you have?"

He looked over his shoulder. "Thirty-seven, including the partners." But he stopped and turned to me again. "Sorry. Thirty-six."

I assumed the miscount included Ted.

Tucker picked up his pace and seemed to have plenty of energy in each step. He'd nod and wave as he walked past each office along the way.

We came to the end of the hall, and he walked straight into an office I assumed was his. But I stopped and looked in just to the left of his door. The lights were off. It appeared to be undisturbed.

"Ted's office," Tucker said from behind his desk. "Nobody's wanted to go in there since..." He stopped, looked down at his desk, and didn't finish. He took a moment, then looked up at me, still in the doorway. "Have a seat, unless you prefer to stand?"

I stepped toward his desk, looked around. A framed diploma from the Massachusetts Institute of Technology caught my eye. "Did you graduate with Ted?"

Tucker nodded. "That's where we met. In fact, we started this company before we even left. We were still undergrads... ready to take on the world."

"Yeah? That's pretty good."

"Well, we didn't technically start up then. I mean, we didn't make money." He huffed out a slight laugh. "We're still working on that part." He turned, looked at a framed photo of himself with Ted and another man, on the wall just a few feet from his MIT diploma. "It all started on a cocktail napkin. Just like they say in the movies." He pressed his lips tight together and shook his head. "It'll never be the same without him." He played with a pen between his fingers and shifted his eyes down.

I kept quiet for a moment.

Tucker looked up at me. "I'm sorry. It's just... it's been a tough week." He leaned back in his chair. "So what can I do for you?"

"I told you on the phone I'm investigating what happened."

Tucker nodded. "I know. But I'm not sure I understand. It was clearly suicide. I've personally spoken to someone at the sheriff's office more than once. And it looks like there's no question." He looked me right in the eye. "Ted was under a lot of pressure." He leaned forward and picked up the pen, twisted it between both hands in front of him. "Not only was there a lot going on here, but his personal life..." He looked up at me. "I don't know how much I should get into any of it, but... did Lynn hire you?"

I looked back at him but didn't answer. "What about things here? I imagine there's been quite an impact on the business?"

Tucker took a moment before he answered, then nodded. "We're holding our own."

"Holding your own? That doesn't sound good."

Tucker placed the pen down and took a moment before he looked up at me again. "If you're here because you want to know if this business could've been what caused Ted to take his own life..." He nodded. "I'd have to say yes. But like I said, he had pressure coming at him from all sides."

I shook my head. "That might be my question if I believed Ted took his own life. But it's not. I'd like to know more about this offer you have to purchase this company. I understand it was pretty substantial, and perhaps some people—maybe even you—weren't happy Ted wouldn't sign off on it."

I could see on Tucker's face he didn't like that at all.

"That is proprietary information. Who told you anything about that? It's not even public."

"How much was it for?" I said, not about to let up.

"Did you not hear what I just said? I don't care what kind of private detective you think you are... I'm not going to share anything with you." He paused. "Did Lynn tell you about it?"

I shook my head. "That's proprietary information." I smirked back at him.

Tucker stood from his desk. "I'm sorry, but I don't have time for this. I have work to do." He walked past me and stood by the doorway.

I stood from the chair. "I'd like to say I'm surprised to see you this upset about a simple question. But I guess I somewhat expected it."

He took a step toward me and seemed to expand his chest a bit. I almost asked him how much he could bench.

"I don't appreciate whatever it is you're trying to imply."

"I'm sorry," I said. "I didn't need to imply anything. I actually prefer to be a little more forward." I walked past him toward the door, then turned and looked down at him, no more than a foot between us. "What I should have done is come right out and say it's my understanding you wanted to sell... and Ted did not. And I would have to guess that created quite a bit of tension between the two of you?"

I felt a presence behind me and turned toward the doorway. A man in a security guard's uniform stepped toward me. His arms were much thicker than Tucker's. Maybe they were workout buddies.

I said to Tucker, "Business can't be too bad; you can afford a security guard."

He gave the security guard a nod. "Show Mr. Walsh the door."

The guard reached for me and grabbed my arm, but I yanked it away. "I don't believe 'show him the door' means you can put your sweaty palms on my arm."

A second guard came up behind the first and stood staring at me over his friend's shoulder.

I turned to Tucker and put up two fingers. "Two security guards." I nodded my approval. "Not bad."

They both reached through the doorway and grabbed each of my arms.

I didn't resist, knowing it wouldn't help much. Not with the two goons, both built like a couple of Mack trucks. I turned and looked at Tucker, watching me from just outside his doorway. "I'll be in touch," I said.

Alex was at her desk at our office when I walked in an hour after I said I would. She looked up at me from behind her computer but didn't say a word for a moment. She shifted her eyes back to the screen. "I thought you'd be more anxious to see the footage," she said.

"I am. I just... sorry I didn't make it over last night. I had some things I had to take care of."

She rolled her eyes.

"I went to see Tucker Dennison at Chemcore Science," I said.

"Ted's partner?"

I nodded. "He was a pleasant man until I asked about the deal Jack said they had on the table to sell. He didn't like that I'd asked. In fact, he was surprised I knew anything about it. Said it wasn't public knowledge. And when I wouldn't tell him how I knew about it, he called a couple of security guards in to escort me out of the building."

Alex shook her head. "Can't you play the game just a little? You always have to go for the throat."

I laughed. "I hardly went for his throat. I asked the question, and he didn't like it."

She stared back at me, like she didn't believe me.

"That's the truth." I walked to the coffeepot and poured myself a coffee. "His knee-jerk reaction was odd, if you ask me. Certainly looks suspicious, the way he got so upset."

I stepped behind Alex and looked over her shoulder at the screen. "So what'd you find?" She had a frame paused on a shot of the hotel's entrance.

She tapped a key on her laptop and let the video run. "This goes back to the morning."

"The morning before?"

Alex nodded. "Before he checked in that afternoon. I wanted to see if I could find Olivia on her way out." She turned and gave me a quick look, then pointed to the screen. "You can see her here, heading for the garage." She clicked the keyboard to speed up the footage. It was a lot busier earlier than it was when I was there in the evening, people buzzing back and forth through the lobby and in and out of the hotel. "What time did you get there?" she said.

"A little before five."

She stopped the video. "Well, then, what is he doing there?" She pointed to the screen and looked back at me. "That's him, isn't it?"

I leaned closer. "It's not that clear, but... I think you're right. What time is that?"

"One fifty."

"He was there already? But I followed him from his house."

We watched him walk alone into the lounge. Alex sped up the video and slowed it down again when he left.

"He must've gone home, got his things and left again. Maybe to throw off Lynn."

"I see him there. But it doesn't make much sense, does it?"

Alex shrugged. "Why not? He must've met someone there. But there's not a camera in the lounge, so it's impossible to know who he was in there with, from the footage."

"Didn't you see anybody leave?" I said.

"A few people. In fact"—she clicked a key on the laptop again and ran the video forward—"you'll see him talking to someone else, but the other person's standing behind the column. You can barely see the back of someone's head. It may be a woman, but it's impossible to know for sure."

"It's almost like whoever it is knows there's a camera."

Alex shook her head. "I don't know about that. I think it's just bad luck.

We both watched for another few moments until Ted turned and walked away, passed under the camera on his way toward the front entrance.

"Well, then, I guess we'll be forced to go get a drink." I walked over toward my desk. "See if whoever's behind the bar at the hotel lounge might know who was in there with Ted."

Chapter 7

IT WAS A LITTLE past two o'clock. Alex and I ordered drinks from the gray-haired woman behind the bar, at the lounge of the same hotel where Ted had fallen to his death.

She poured herself a soda into a shot glass from the soda gun, took a sip, and leaned with one hand on the cooler just below where she stood. "Are you here from out of town?"

I turned and noticed a man and a woman in one of the booths toward the back of the lounge, kissing.

"Do I even need to tell them to get a room?" I said.

The bartender laughed.

"No, we just wanted to stop at the lounge. I heard you pour a good Jack Daniels," I said. I took a sip from my glass.

She smiled and started to walk away. "Well, my name's April, if you need anything else."

Alex spoke up. "Excuse me?"

April turned. "Yes, sweetie?"

"I'm Alex." She gave a nod toward me. "And this is Henry."

I said, "Do you work this time every day?"

She gave us both a somewhat suspicious look, then after a moment shook her head. "Not every day. It depends on the schedule. Some nights, but..."

I said, "Were you here the night of the incident last week?"

She gave a slight tilt to her head. "The incident?"

"The man who fell from the balcony?" I said.

She closed her eyes, looked down toward the bar, and shook her head. "Hard to believe. Never heard of anything like that happening here. Been here almost seven years. I wasn't here though. I was supposed to work... but glad I didn't. Had to swap shifts with a girlfriend of mine. She was here." Again, she shook her head, then looked toward the couple in the booth. "Freaks me out just thinking about it."

Alex leaned down on the bar. "You were here during the day?"

She nodded. "Are you with the sheriff's office or something?" She narrowed her eyes. "I already told you people all I knew about—"

"We're not with the sheriff's office," I said. "But I actually knew the victim."

She stared back at me with a slow nod. "Oh. I'm sorry."

53

"I didn't know him well. I mean, it's a tragedy, but..." I looked over my shoulder again, made sure the only other two people there were occupied with their own business. And they were. "Do *you* know who the man was? Who fell?" I said.

"I'm not even sure I know what the man looked like." She nodded toward the stool next to me. "He could've been seated right there next to you, I wouldn't have known."

Alex pulled out her phone and turned the screen to the woman. "This is him."

She pulled a pair of reading glasses from her shirt pocket, held them up to her eyes and stared back at Ted Parker's photo. She kept her eyes there for a moment, then shook her head. "I don't think so. Looks like a handsome man. I would've remembered him."

I said, "He was in here that afternoon, right around this time."

She shrugged. "I'm sorry."

Alex looked at her phone and tapped the screen, turned it back toward the woman. "Do you recognize this woman?"

She'd just pulled off her glasses but put them back on, leaned toward the phone in Alex's hand. She looked at Alex, then turned to me and nodded. "She'd been in here. More than once."

"Alone?" I said.

She pulled her glasses off her eyes again and slipped them into her shirt pocket. "If you're not cops, then why're you asking these kinds of questions?" She shook her head. "I'm just here, making enough money to keep my head above water. I don't need to be involved in any—"

"We're private investigators," I said, then pulled my card out and placed it on the bar in front of her. "We're just trying to put some pieces together for something we're working on."

"Something that has to do with that poor man's death?" she said. She filled her glass again with soda and took a sip, then crossed her arms over her chest. She kept the glass in her hand. "She was in here alone as far as I could tell." But then she squinted her eyes and turned her head, looked toward the floor like she was thinking. She looked up and said, "You know what? I think I'm wrong. Because I came in early, before the lounge even opens, and I'm almost certain she was in here with someone. Even if we're closed, the guests'll come in sometimes, sit in one of the booths and have a coffee."

Alex said, "Alone?"

"No. She was with a man."

I turned to the woman. "You just said a moment ago she was alone. So I just want to make sure you're—"

55

"Her hair's a little different in that photo. So it took me a moment to put it all together. But, yes… I'm sure." She straightened herself up and reached down into the dishwasher, pulled out a couple of glasses and slid them onto the rack over her head. "A lot of people come through here. I don't mean nothing by saying it, but I don't pay attention to every one of 'em who walks through that door."

I said, "What about the man? Was it Mr. Parker?"

"Who?"

"Ted Parker. The man who died?"

"No. Not based on that picture you showed me. But, like I said, I'm just not certain."

· · · • • • • • · ·

I'd left three messages for Olivia Peckham, and she still hadn't returned my calls. But rather than wait for her to call me back, Alex and I left the hotel and drove out to a wooded neighborhood in Crawford, where Olivia lived.

The way Jack described her, she was very successful and liked to show it. But her house was a modest-sized brick home with a two-car garage. Nothing fancy at all but looked to have plenty of land. You could just about see the other homes on either side of her property.

We parked in the driveway and walked up the stairs. Alex and I stood on the top step, and I rang the doorbell. But nobody answered. I rang it again and tried to look inside through one of the panes of glass, but the lights were off, and there wasn't much I could see.

There didn't appear to be anyone home.

I turned and walked down the steps.

"Should we wait?" Alex said.

I shook my head. "For what? Who knows where she is." I looked down at my phone. "I wish she'd at least return my calls."

"Maybe she's avoiding us?"

We stood in the driveway and looked around the neighborhood until I spotted an older man in the yard next door. He had a hose in his hand, watering flowers. He looked at us through the woods between their homes. But he turned away when I looked at him.

"Maybe the old man knows where to find her." I walked across Olivia's lawn toward him, ducked under a branch, and said, "My name's Henry." I pointed with my thumb toward Olivia's house. "Any idea if she's around? I've been trying to get in touch with her, but..."

He turned and walked away from me without a word, reached down for the spigot on the side of his house, then turned off the water. He rolled up the hose. "Are you a friend of Olivia's?" He pulled the rolled-up hose onto a hook next to the spigot.

Alex walked up behind me, and the man's eyes lit up. She reached her hand out for his. "Hi, I'm Alex."

He wiped his hands on his shorts, then shook her hand. "Hi, Alex. I'm Albert. Albert Conlon." He looked her up and down.

"Hi, Albert. Nice to meet you." She nodded my way. "This is Henry. We were just checking up on Olivia. She won't return our calls. We thought we'd come by to see if she was home, but..." Alex shook her head and turned toward Olivia's house. "I just hope she's all right."

Albert looked toward Olivia's house. "You sure she's not on the road? I know she travels a lot with work." He turned his eyes to Alex. "I'm sure you know how busy she is."

"We just want to be sure she's okay," I said.

He looked back and forth from me to Alex. "You said she didn't answer her phone?"

Alex shook her head. "And she always calls me back."

The old man scratched the top of his head, then looked behind him toward his own house. "Well, since you're a friend of hers..." He again looked Alex up and down. "And you seem to be nice enough... we actually keep a spare key she gave us. In case there's ever an emergency."

Alex gave me a quick glance, then shifted her eyes to Albert. "Maybe we could have a quick peek inside, make sure there's nothing out of order?" She watched him as he seemed to think for a moment.

I gave him a friendly nod, pointed to Alex. "She's always worried about her friends. Makes me drive her all the way out here just because she won't call her back."

Albert nodded after a brief pause. "All right. Let me go get that key." He turned and walked toward the garage and disappeared inside.

"What are we expecting to find in there?" Alex said.

I took a moment before I answered. "I don't know. Better than waiting for her to call us back, isn't it?"

The old man came back out through the garage, held the key up in front of him and dangled it toward Alex. "Here you go." He handed her the key and pulled a piece of paper from his pocket. "This is the code for the alarm, but she doesn't always keep it on."

"We'll bring it right back," she said, and we both turned and started toward the house.

But Albert started to follow after us.

"You might want to stay behind," I said. "Maybe she's sick. A man your age…"

He nodded and smiled. "Just make sure you bring the key back, all right? Just give it to my wife if she answers the door."

The three of us all looked toward the street. A black car drove by us. It looked like a Lincoln or Cadillac, but I wasn't up on cars. Not the new American ones that only seemed to get bigger every year.

Albert turned, and I noticed his eyes followed the car. "I don't know who it is, but whoever it is drives by two or three times a day. At least for the past few days."

We all watched until the black car turned the corner and disappeared.

· · · • • • • · · ·

There was no need to disarm the alarm at Olivia's house. In fact, when we walked in, we both found it odd that only the doorknob was locked. The dead bolt was not.

"Nice place," Alex said from behind me.

The house was older, but it didn't appear that way on the inside. It appeared to have been completely remodeled, with a modern look inside much different from the old brick exterior.

"I'll be honest," I said. "I'm not exactly sure what we're looking for." I pushed open a set of double doors in the hallway and looked inside a laundry area. I turned to look at Alex but she was gone. "Where'd you go?" I said.

But she didn't answer.

"Alex?"

"I'm in here."

I followed her voice down the hall and walked into what looked like a home office. I sniffed into the air. "What's that smell?"

Alex turned to me and nodded toward the desk. On top was a mirror with white lines of powder on top. "Looks like someone's into cocaine." She stepped around the desk to the other side of it. She gasped. "Henry!" Her eyes were drawn to the floor.

I stepped around the desk and followed her gaze to a woman's lifeless body on the floor. Her eyes were open, her face blue. She had dried blood under her nose.

"Is it her?" I said.

Alex looked at me but didn't answer. She didn't have to.

We both knew it was her.

Olivia Peckham was dead.

Chapter 8

DETECTIVE MIKE STONE WAS far from happy to run into me a second time within a week concerning a dead body he had to deal with.

"It's nothing more than an overdose," he said, matter-of-factly, and didn't have any interest in hearing what else we had to say. "And if you think I'm in a position to defend you, I'm not exactly sure what to say." He shook his head and watched as the stretcher with the body bag containing Olivia Peckham's body was wheeled past us toward the driveway. He started to walk away.

Alex said, "Mike, listen. We were only here to talk to her. The last thing we expected was—"

"You broke into this woman's house, Alex. Is that what you do? Break into someone's house, to talk to them?"

I held up the key. "I don't think it's technically breaking and entering when you have a key. Maybe just unlocking and entering." I nodded toward the old man watching us with his wife next to him, both of them in front of their house, but somewhat visible through the trees.

Mike turned to them. "Nice to have neighbors who watch your house, hand out your key to anyone who asks for it."

"It's not the old man's fault," Alex said. "We kind of told him Olivia was a friend."

Mike pulled a cigarette from inside his coat pocket, gave it a light and took a drag.

Alex gave a slight tilt to her head as she watched Mike exhale into the air. "I thought you quit?"

He nodded. "I did." He took another drag and exhaled. "I quit all the time." He again started to walk away but stopped and turned to me. "Tell me one more time. What makes you think this woman's overdose is somehow related to the suicide at the hotel?"

"She was married to Ted Parker's brother."

Mike took another drag and took a step closer to me. "Jack Parker?"

"You know him?"

Mike shook his head. "Spoke to him on the phone for two minutes after his brother's death. He called me, asked if we were sure it was suicide."

"What'd you tell him?"

"What do you mean 'what did I tell him?' We have no reason to believe it was anything else."

"How about the fact Olivia Peckham was at the Baymeadow Hotel, checked out the day of Ted Parker's death?"

Mike narrowed his eyes. "How'd you know that?" He dropped the cigarette on the ground, then smashed it out with his foot. He picked it up and held on to it.

"I asked the woman at the hotel."

Mike looked around, then stepped closer to me, his voice lowered. "Are you going to tell me who you're working for?"

"Technically?" I shook my head. "Just doing our civic duty to ensure the sheriff's office doesn't get another one wrong."

Mike squinted his eyes. I could hear something come from within him, like a deep growl vibrating up from his throat. "Maybe you oughta find something better to do with your free time," he said. He took a step closer to me and we stood eye to eye with each other.

Alex stepped between me and Mike. "Come on, Mike," she said. "You know we were working for Mrs. Parker. We're just doing a little extra, that's all. No harm in that, is there?"

"If you're getting in the way of letting me do my job, there is."

I watched the coroner's vehicle pull out from the driveway.

"So, let me guess," Mike said. "You think there's some kind of connection to this woman's death and Ted Parker's suicide? You don't think a half-snorted line of coke three feet from the body had something to do with it?"

"I don't know if there's a connection. But, she was in that hotel. It looks like they were doing business together. And Olivia, I believe, was an investor in his company."

Mike stared back at me, then looked up toward the open door of the house. Another investigator had called out for him. He turned and walked up the stairs and disappeared inside without another word.

My phone rang but I didn't recognize the number. I answered anyway. "Henry Walsh."

"Hi, uh... this is April, from the lounge at the Baymeadow Hotel. You said to call you if I thought of anything else. And I just checked the slips from that afternoon when you asked if that woman was here." She paused, and I realized I hadn't said a word.

"April?"

"Yes, well, I'm friends with the manager here. And I told her you were in here, and that you're a private investigator. I hope that's okay?"

"It's fine. But what did you—"

"Well we had a slow day," she said, "so I thought we could try to help you out. And I have a name for you."

"A name?"

"Yeah, my manager knows the woman you were talking about. Even knew her name, Olivia Peckham. Right?"

"Yes, that's her name. But..."

"Well, this man paid for the drinks. The name on his credit card was L. J. Hoover."

"Hoover?"

"Yes, that's what it says on the slip."

"LJ? The initials? No full name?"

"That's what it says. LJ."

I turned to Alex and held the phone against my chest. "L. J. Hoover, one of Ted's partners. He bought drinks for Olivia, according to our friend April." I put the phone back up to my ear. "Anything else your friend might've noticed?"

"No, I don't think so."

"I'm glad you called, April. We really appreciate you following up."

"I hope it helps," she said.

Mike had already walked inside the house while I was on the phone, so Alex and I started for the Jeep.

I stepped inside with the phone up to my ear. "One thing, April. If you wouldn't mind, could you keep this quiet?

Especially if someone from the sheriff's office comes around asking any more questions. Just don't mention anything about me."

"Sure thing," she said. "I understand. But do you want me to call you if I hear anything?"

"That would be great. Thank you." I hung up the phone and turned to Alex in the passenger seat. "Let's see if we can track down L. J. Hoover."

I started to back out into the street and had to avoid the parked cars all around us, most unmarked from the sheriff's office. But I stopped and turned to look behind us toward the road. A car drove past, and I was almost sure it was the same black vehicle we saw earlier: a Cadillac.

I decided to follow it.

Chapter 9

WE TURNED INTO WALTER Jones Historical Park.

Alex had her new Glock resting on her lap.

The Cadillac turned left.

I turned right and parked at the far end of the parking lot. Far enough away but close enough that we could see who it was if anyone got out.

But the Cadillac pulled into a parking space on the other side of a white van. Our view was blocked.

After a few moments, the window on the passenger side of the van went down. A man wearing dark sunglasses and a baseball cap stuck his head out and looked right at us. He stepped out of the van and walked around to the other side where the Cadillac was parked.

I turned to look at Alex. "Should we drive over there?"

She shook her head. "Probably not a good idea."

Three men, all wearing sunglasses and baseball caps, walked around the van and started coming our way.

"Oh shit," I said. I turned the key in the ignition. And as soon as the engine started, all three men started to run toward us. I yanked the stick into reverse and squealed the tires as I cut the wheel and fishtailed toward the exit. But a young woman was walking across the lot pushing a baby stroller in front of us. She had a phone in her hand and seemed to be oblivious we were headed right for her.

I slammed on my brakes, and the woman looked up, screamed, and dropped her phone. Her eyes were wide open but her gaze wasn't on me. She looked past us, and in the rearview mirror I saw the three men, guns drawn, closing in.

"Get down!" I yelled to both Alex and the woman. Then I jammed the shifter into reverse and slammed my foot down on the gas. I was headed right for the three men. They separated, and two of them dove out of the way. The third stayed on his feet and fired a shot but missed.

I cut the wheel and clipped him with the right rear quarter, knocked him straight back a good ten feet onto the asphalt. I looked ahead to make sure the young woman was all right. I didn't see her anywhere and had to assume she was safe.

Alex lifted her 9mm and turned around in the passenger seat.

I ducked when another shot was fired. I had no idea where it came from. The man I hit was still down, but the other two were nowhere to be seen. I yelled to Alex, "Stay down!" then shifted into drive and slammed my foot down on the pedal. We headed for the exit but jumped the curb and cut into oncoming traffic on Mandarin Road.

"They're behind us," Alex said.

I looked in the rearview and saw the black Cadillac coming fast up the rear of my Jeep. But my eyes shifted to the gas gauge.

"What's wrong?" she said. "I mean, aside from the fact we were just shot at, and now being chased."

I looked at the gas gauge. "I don't know how far this gas is going to take us."

"You're out of gas?" she yelled. "Are you serious?"

"Am I serious? I wasn't expecting to be involved in a car chase. We're going to have to pull off somewhere. There's a shopping center up ahead. Maybe we can lose them in there."

A loud bang went off somewhere in the Jeep.

Alex yelled, "They just shot at us!"

The Cadillac was right behind us. I couldn't shake it loose. I jerked the wheel and pulled into the parking lot of the shopping center with a Big Moe's Furniture Warehouse toward the back. I drove between the long rows of cars, doing a good fifty miles an hour. I didn't want to get either of us shot, but I also didn't want to kill someone walking across the lot.

I took another hard turn down another row, and saw an open space toward the far end. I slammed down the gas pedal. "As soon as I park, we'll run inside. I can't imagine they'd go in there with their guns drawn."

"You don't know that," Alex said.

I turned into the parking space. "Go!"

We both ran and stayed low. The Cadillac came roaring toward us and stopped just outside the entrance.

Alex and I made it inside.

A woman dressed much nicer than the customers came toward us with a big smile on her face. "Welcome to Moe's Furniture Warehouse. May I help you find what you're looking for?"

Neither one of us answered and stepped past her, picked up our pace, and ran toward the back of the store. I looked back over my shoulder and saw two of the men walk through the sliding door at the entrance.

We turned down one of the aisles. But when we got to the end, I turned right and started to run. I stopped and looked behind me but Alex wasn't there. She was running in the opposite direction along the back wall of the store. I couldn't yell for her, not unless I wanted either of us to get noticed.

A shot was fired, and the building was filled with screams.

Right then I regretted not being armed. I didn't love guns. I preferred doing work without them. And, normally, they weren't necessary. But if I was going to be on the receiving end of a bullet, it would only make sense to have a fighting chance.

Another shot was fired, and it didn't sound like it was far away.

A man said, "What the hell are you shooting at that for?" I saw a couple of swinging steel doors with Employees Only printed on a sign above them. I ran through the doors and ended up in what looked like a stockroom. It was twice the size of the rest of the store and loaded with furniture and boxes and mattresses stacked twenty feet high.

I wanted to yell out for Alex, but I'd only put her in danger. I didn't even know if it'd be a good idea to send her a text. But I knew she was smart enough to turn off the ringer. At least I'd hoped she was.

I crouched down behind the mattresses and typed into my phone:

Are you okay?

I stared at the screen and waited for a response. Please answer.

My phone vibrated.

I don't know. I'm somewhere in the stockroom at a garage door, but it's locked.

She couldn't have been far from me. I didn't see anyone else around, likely disappeared when the shots were fired. And I was sure someone called the cops.

It was quiet. Too quiet.

I stayed ducked behind the stack of mattresses, but then heard a young man's voice.

"Can I help you?" Then a cry. "No! Please! Please don't shoot!"

It was followed by shoes slapping against the concrete floor. Whoever it was ran away. Luckily, nobody stopped him. I heard doors crash open, then the same man's voice. "Somebody back there's got a gun!"

But there was silence. I was sure the building had emptied out. Apparently, he was the only person in the place who hadn't heard the shots.

My phone buzzed again.

Alex sent another text:

Where are you?

But before I could answer, I heard the all-too-familiar click. I didn't turn to look but right away raised my hands and straightened up onto my feet.

"Let's go," said a voice from behind me.

Sirens grew louder somewhere outside the building. But they weren't close enough.

The man said, "I got 'im. Bring the car around back. And hurry. Cops are on their way."

I turned and looked over my shoulder. The first thing I saw was the gun.

"Keep your eyes going the other way." He pressed the muzzle into the back of my skull. "I'm not afraid to pull the trigger, if you'd like to try me."

I thought it'd be smart to listen. He grabbed me by the shirt and pulled me back out from behind the mattresses, the muzzle still pressed against my head. He pushed me ahead, and we walked toward a large garage door. I wondered if Alex could have been that close, but there was no way it was the only door.

I faced the door, and the man reached past me, pressed a button, and the door started to open.

He looked outside and I spun around, hoping to knock the gun from his hand.

But he was faster than I'd hoped. He stepped back and I missed him entirely. He jumped on me and drove his fist into my ribs, then swung down hard with the pistol in his hand. He cracked it down on my head, then struck me again, caught me right above the eye.

I felt the warmth of my own blood come down my face. I tried to take a swing, but I had nothing in me. I saw stars right away, and he connected one more time. I fell to the ground, looked up and saw the black Cadillac backed up to the opening. Two men grabbed me and dragged me toward the open trunk and tossed me inside. I tried to push myself out. But something I didn't see coming struck my skull. The men in front of me became a blur, and everything went dark.

Chapter 10

I WOKE UP TO a musty smell, with my hands and feet tied to a small metal chair inside a dimly lit room, with unfinished walls and a stained concrete floor. The light over my head came from a single bulb, although light also slipped from underneath a door.

There was a folding table in the room just a few feet away from me. It looked like there was a phone on top, and I wondered if it was mine. I tried to slide myself in the chair but a chain wrapped around the legs and attached to a vertical post behind me kept me from moving the chair anywhere. If the chair were wood, I could've tried harder to break free.

I felt pain in my neck when I turned to the door. "Hello? Anybody out there?" My brain was foggy, to say the least. And I was just starting to remember what had happened. My face hurt. I looked down at my pants and saw the dried stains from my own blood.

I tried to move my hands, but the rope around my wrists was tight. Then I tried to push myself from the floor with my feet even though they were tied together. "Hey! Anybody hear me out there?" I yelled.

Someone was on the other side of the door. The knob turned, and sunlight filled the room. I squinted and turned away as if it would make me blind. I looked back and saw a dark figure standing in the doorway, but it was almost impossible to make out the face with the bright sunlight all around it.

"Would you mind helping untie me?" I said, then nodded toward the table. "And if that's my phone, I need to make a call."

The figure moved closer and the door slammed closed.

A large man stood in silence with a Ronald Reagan mask over his face. His sleeveless arms were thick and long and packed with muscle.

I had to keep my head turned to see him. "Mr. President? What a surprise, although I thought you were already dead."

"Shut up," he said, his voice muffled behind the cheap plastic mask. He pulled a gun from his waist but held it down by his side.

"What are you planning to do with that?" I said. "If you're planning to kill me, I'd at least like to know what for."

He raised the gun and pointed toward me. "I'm pretty sure I told you to shut your mouth."

"Well, I'd just like to warn you... there are people out right now who are looking for me."

"Is that right?" he said. He took a step closer. "How about we make a deal?"

"Let's make a deal!" I said, doing my best to put on the voice of a game show host.

"You want to see your girlfriend alive again?"

I shuffled in the chair and tried to move, but it was no use. "What did you do? Where is she?" I yelled out as loud as I could. "Alex!"

"Listen to me," the man said. "I'll make it easy for you. If you don't stop investigating what happened to Ted Parker, you'll have to make sure you never take your eyes off of your girlfriend, Annie, again."

"Annie?" I said. Now I was confused.

The man nodded. "Isn't she your girlfriend?"

I didn't answer.

"Well, you keep at it and she'll be dead. And you'll be the only one to blame." The man laughed, then stepped toward me. He looked down at his gun, ran his fingers along the barrel. "Now, what about that blonde partner of yours? Sounds like you're more worried about her than the girlfriend?"

"Where is she?" I said. I looked around and continued to work the rope around my wrists.

The man didn't answer me.

"So what are you? Just some hired thug getting a few hundred bucks to knock me around, send me a message? You probably don't even know who Ted Parker is." I tried to look into the man's eyes. "What'd you do, run an ad on Craigslist? Under criminal services?"

"I know exactly who he is." He let out a slight laugh. "Or... I should say who he *was*."

"Are you the one who threw him off the balcony?"

He shook his head, and the mask slid to the side. He straightened it out on his face. That's when I noticed the tattoo on the back of his wrist—a double red cross.

"Who killed him isn't important," the man said.

"So you're admitting he was killed?"

He lifted his gun and put the muzzle up against my face, pressed it into my cheek, just under my eye. "The only thing I'm telling you is to walk away from this case, or you'll have not one... but two dead girlfriends. You'll be all alone." He laughed behind the mask.

"How am I supposed to walk away when you've got me tied up to a chair."

"You know what I mean, smartass." He put his hand under his mask and whistled. The door opened and two men walked in, each with a gun in their hand and masks over their faces. The shorter one had a mask of Bill Clinton. The other—tall and skinny—wore a Hillary Clinton mask.

"I believe you know how this is going to work?" the man said, still holding the gun pressed up against my face. But he eased up on the pressure, then stepped back from me.

"Actually, I have no idea," I said. "But what's with the presidential masks? That's the best you could come up with? Reagan and the Clintons? A little behind the times..."

The man swung the hand holding the gun and struck me across the face. "You talk too much," he said. "Now I need you to listen. If we let you go, and you continue to investigate Ted Parker's death, your girlfriends will pay the price. It's pretty simple. Do you understand? You make the wrong move, and their blood will be on your hands."

The other two men stood on either side of me and laughed.

The big man with the Reagan mask gave Bill Clinton a nod. He turned and walked toward the door. "I was afraid you weren't going to take me seriously." He opened the door and sunlight, again, filled the room. I couldn't see through the bright sunlight, but I could tell he was looking back at me. "I'd heard you could be a bit stubborn," he said.

I continued working my hands and knew I didn't have much time. Reagan walked out and closed the door behind him.

But he came right back a moment later and had Annie in his grasp. Her mouth was covered with duct tape. Her hands were tied together behind her back. Reagan slammed the door closed behind him.

Annie had tears running down her face.

"She has nothing to do with this!" I yelled. "Let her go. You can take it out on me."

Reagan pushed her away from him. The shorter, Bill Clinton character, caught her as she stumbled into his arms. He pushed her down onto the floor next to me.

Annie looked up at me, her eyes filled with tears.

"I'm so sorry," I said to her. It was all I could say.

The man in the Hillary mask went out the door and came back a minute later with more rope in his hands. He crouched down next to Annie and tied her to the bottom of my chair. Reagan lifted his foot and pushed me until I tipped over in the chair. My head landed in Annie's lap.

She screamed from behind the gag in her mouth.

The three men stood over us and laughed.

"Can't you at least take that out of her mouth," I said, trying to get myself in a position so I wasn't crushing her.

Reagan said, "You mean, so she can scream?" He shook his head. "No can do." He gave his short friend a nod, and the man handed him a piece of rope. The two Clintons crouched down and lifted me so the chair was back on all fours.

Reagan stepped toward me with the rope and reached around behind my head, most likely to wrap the rope across my mouth.

But when my chair fell to the ground, it had loosened up the rope just enough to where I'd managed to get my hands free.

Before Reagan had a chance to tie the rope around my mouth, I ripped it from his hands and flipped it behind his head. I tied it around once, then yanked him toward me and drove my head into his face. I felt something explode behind the mask. I pulled the rope tighter.

Blood came down his neck. His masked face was no more than four inches from mine. I could smell his breath. He tried to grip the rope with his fingers and pull it from his throat, but I wouldn't let up. I pulled tighter.

He gagged behind the mask and struggled, trying to get me to loosen my grip.

I was hesitant to let go of the rope, but his gun was right there in front of me, in the waist of his pants. So I squeezed the rope together with one hand and used the other to grab the gun. I pulled the trigger and fired just as the man with the Hillary mask stepped toward me to help his friend.

He took a bullet in the chest and dropped down to the concrete floor.

I hadn't let go of the rope around Reagan's neck and held it with all my might and twisted it around my fist.

The man choked behind the mask, and I stuck the gun under his chin.

But Bill Clinton pulled his gun out and turned it toward me. "Let him go!" he yelled.

I shook my head. "You shoot me," I said, "and the Gipper gets it... right up in his tiny brain." I glanced at Annie out of the corner of my eye. "Let her go, or your friend dies." I twisted the rope and kept it tight. "Untie her. Now!"

The short one stared at me through his mask, then looked down at his bloodied friend on the floor. He held the gun on me but appeared frozen and unsure what his next move should be.

The man behind the Reagan mask squeezed words out from his choking throat. "Un... tie... her."

Clinton didn't react right away but finally nodded and tucked his gun in his pants. He crouched down next to Annie and removed a knife from his pocket. He slid the blade of the knife back and forth and started to cut through the rope around her ankles.

I looked down at her. "Was there anyone else outside?"

She shook her head, then shrugged.

"Remove that thing from her mouth so she can breathe."

"Don't worry," I said to her. "We'll be okay." I pulled the man with the Reagan mask closer and pressed the muzzle of the gun deeper into the skin of his neck.

But the big man still felt he had the upper hand. "You're... making... a... big... mistake," he said. He could barely get out a word. His breath came through the mask.

"How awful," I said. "What did you eat for lunch? Salami?"

Annie's feet were finally free again. The short man with the Clinton mask got up, crouched behind her, and removed the rope from her wrists. He pulled the duct tape from her mouth and she let out a gasp, sucking in whatever air she could with fast and deep breaths.

"Now, give her your gun," I said.

The man's eyes were wider than the slits in his mask. He looked at his friend with his head practically in my lap.

I pressed the gun hard under the big guy's chin. "Tell him to give her his gun!" I yelled.

He nodded and his eyes went to his friend. "Give... it... to... her."

The man pulled the gun from his pants and handed it to Annie.

It was clear she didn't know which end she was supposed to grip. But she must've seen enough movies, and after a moment figured out it would be best if she pointed the barrel away from her and toward the man.

"Now give her your knife," I said.

Clinton handed her his knife. He raised his hands into the air. But before anyone could react, he jumped over his bloody friend on the floor and reached for the door. He ripped it open and disappeared into the streaks of sunlight bolting in from outside.

I twisted the rope and threw the big man down to the floor. His mask fell off, and I could see him now. But I didn't recognize the face. I held the gun on him with both hands. "You move, and I'll shoot." I glanced at Annie from the corner of my eye. "Use that knife and cut this rope from my feet."

She put the gun she held down on the floor and crouched in front of me. She leaned down and worked the knife back and forth to cut through the rope.

The big man was on his back on the floor. He closed his eyes and rubbed his throat with both hands. The rope had burned the skin around his neck. He glanced at his bloodied friend's body next to him. "You have no idea who you're messing with," he said. He rubbed his throat.

"Why don't you go ahead and tell me who I'm messing with?" I said. My feet were free, and I stepped out of what was left of the rope tied to the legs of the chair.

Annie stood up next to me and I glanced down at the gun on the floor. "Why don't you pick that up," I said.

She nodded without a word and picked it up. "What do you want me to do?"

"Just keep it aimed at him in case he tries something." I pointed the gun at him. "Get up. Let's go. You're going to take me to Alex." I nodded toward the table with the phone on top. "Grab that," I said to Annie. "I think it's mine. Call Alex."

"It's locked," she said.

"One-one-one-one is the password."

"That doesn't sound very secure," she said.

I rolled my eyes and took the phone from her, then wiggled the gun at the man. "Let's go! Get up!"

He got to his feet and took a step toward the door. I took a quick look at Annie, and the man swatted the gun from my hand, pulled open the door, and ran outside.

Gunshots were fired.

"Get down!" I yelled. But another shot rang out before I could get out of the way. The phone flew from my hand and I immediately felt an aching burn.

The bullet had hit the phone and nicked a piece of my hand.

More shots were fired from outside.

Blood poured from my hand. The phone was almost in half and clearly dead. I bent down and picked up the gun with my good mitt and fired what was likely a dangerous shot, through the open door. I yelled to Annie, "Stay here!"

I fired another shot as I ran out the door.

The big man ran away from me, and a white van was taking off ahead of him. It stopped, and he jumped in the passenger side and it took off. The van's wheels spun over the dry dirt, sideswiped the side of the Cadillac, then kept going down what looked like a dirt road and disappeared into the trees.

Chapter 11

We stood in the hot sun and walked toward the Cadillac with the side smashed in.

"Do you have any idea where we are?" Annie said. It was one of the few words I'd heard come from her mouth since the men had disappeared.

I pulled open the door and reached my hand past the steering wheel for the ignition. "Hopefully, they left some keys." I pulled down the visor and looked under the driver's seat. Nothing.

I stepped out of the car and walked back into the small concrete building with the windows boarded up. The body of the man I'd shot was in the middle of the floor in a pool of blood. I grabbed him by his shirt and turned him over. I reached into his pockets and felt relieved when I felt a set of keys. I pulled them out and headed back outside.

Annie was still standing by the car.

I held up the keys. "Got 'em."

She walked around to get in the passenger side. "I can't open the door," she said. "It's all smashed over here."

I waved her to come around to my side. "Slide in this way." I held her by the arm and helped her get into the car. "You all right?" I said.

She moved over to the passenger side and settled into the seat. She turned to me and nodded. "I think so."

I turned the ignition and took off down the same road. By the time we got to the end, a wooden fence had clearly been driven through, with broken pieces of wood scattered on the ground. I turned onto a paved road. I was still unsure exactly where we were. I felt Annie watching me from the passenger seat.

"Why am I here?" she said finally. "What did those people want with me?"

I glanced at her but needed to keep my eyes on the road. "You didn't do anything. They must have thought we were together."

"Why would they think that?"

"Because they must've been following me and saw us together at some point. You heard them... all they want me to do is stop the investigation into Ted Parker's death."

Annie looked straight ahead toward the road.

"Don't worry," I said. "I won't let anything happen to you."

·········

We drove in silence for another few miles and had yet to come to a road sign or any indication of where we were.

"You recognize anything around here?" I said.

Annie shook her head. "I'm not even sure we're in Florida."

And just as the words left her mouth, we both spotted the back of a large sign ahead on the other side of the road.

"Can you read that?" I said.

She turned when we passed the sign and looked out the back of the car. "Yeah. It says Okefenokee National Wildlife Refuge."

"We're in Georgia?" I said. But as the words left my mouth, I spotted another sign up ahead. It said, Welcome to Florida.

"Shouldn't we call the police?" Annie said.

I didn't answer. "Right there's Route 23. We're just over the Florida state line."

"Did you hear me?" she said with somewhat of a snap to her voice.

"Oh yeah. Sorry. I heard you. But right now, we just need to get out of Georgia. I'll call when we get back.

Although the truth was, I had no intention of involving the cops.

· · · · · ● · · · ·

We made it to Arlington in little less than an hour and drove to Alex's house. I was worried for most of the ride something had happened to her.

"Whatever happened to pay phones?" I said.

"Why would anyone use a pay phone when we carry phones everywhere we go."

I turned to her. "Neither one of us *has* a phone. I have no way of getting in touch with Alex."

We pulled into Alex's driveway and I had a bad feeling as soon as we arrived. "Shit," I said. "Her Jeep's not here."

"But how do you know she's not inside?" Annie said.

"I don't." I got out and told Annie to wait in the car. I walked up to Alex's house and knocked on the door. But I knew before I did she wasn't there. I waited a couple of moments and knocked again, then walked back to the car and got inside.

"What about one of the neighbors?" Annie said.

I glanced at her and nodded. "Good idea." I shifted the Cadillac into reverse and drove over to Alex's neighbor's house. I pulled into the driveway and shut off the ignition. "You want to wait here?" I said to Annie.

"Are you serious?"

I stared back at her, then pushed open my door. "All right, let's go."

We walked up the front steps, and I knocked on the door.

After a minute or so, an older woman came to the door. She looked at Annie, then me.

"Hi," I said. "I'm a friend of Alex Jepson's, next door. She's not home, but I was wondering if I could use your phone to call her?"

"You want to use my phone to call Alex? You knocked on her door?"

I nodded. "Yes. Her Jeep's not there."

The woman's eyes moved along the side of my face where the blood had dried. "Were you in an accident?" she said. She looked out toward the Cadillac.

I glanced over my shoulder at the side of the car smashed in on the side, with white paint from the van. "Oh, well... sort of. We're okay though."

"Maybe I can call someone for you? The sheriff's office, perhaps?"

"If you don't want us to use your phone, I understand. A couple of strangers. I'm sure we look a bit suspicious. But maybe if you can call her yourself, tell her Henry is at her house?"

Her serious look warmed with a slight smile. "You're Henry?" she said. "Alex has told me so much about you!"

I didn't want to make eye contact with Annie.

The woman pushed open the screen door and stepped back so Annie and I could walk inside. We followed her into the kitchen, and she handed us a cell phone. "Her number's the first one in there. Because of the A in her name." She looked down at my bloodied hand. "Are you sure you don't need a doctor?"

I shook my head. "It's not as bad as it looks." The blood on my hand had dried and I'd already tapped on Alex's number. But it went right to voicemail. My heart pounded in my chest when I heard her voice on the message. It beeped and I said, "Alex, it's me. I'm at your house. Actually, I'm at your neighbor's house. I don't know where you are. And I'm worried. I'm okay, as you can probably tell. I'm going to head over to the office now. So if you get this, try me there. Oh, my phone's not working, which is why I'm on your neighbor's phone." I listened for a moment as if Alex were on the other end.

93

Chapter 12

"So TELL ME AGAIN why your car's at a furniture store?" Annie said, her gaze on me from the passenger seat when I pulled into the parking lot of Big Moe's Furniture Warehouse to get my car.

"This is almost where it all started," I said. "We went by a house to ask someone some questions. Turns out the woman we were looking for is dead. And when we followed a car that drove past the house while we were there, things got turned around. Alex and I ended up running from them." I turned off the engine. "They were shooting at us, so Alex and I ran inside for cover. Those men with the masks... They grabbed me from the back of the warehouse."

Annie said, "Whose house was it?"

"When we saw the car? A woman who might've been involved in Ted Parker's death. But when we got inside her house, she was dead."

Her eyes opened wide. "She was dead?"

"It was made to look like an overdose," I said. "But I'm not convinced it was."

"So you think she was murdered?" Annie said.

I paused, thinking. "I hope to find out." Annie wasn't much different from when I first met her. Untrusting. Defensive. But I guess I couldn't blame her. She never expected to be in this position with her own life at risk. I said, "I promise I will keep you safe."

She laughed. "You say that, but I'm not seeing much proof. You didn't keep your friend safe, did you?"

"Alex?"

Annie shook her head. "No, the woman at the house. The one you said overdosed."

"Oh, she wasn't a friend. I actually had never met her. But I think she knew something, and someone might have gotten to her before she told me anything."

"This is all connected to the man who jumped from the hotel?"

"I told you. He didn't jump." I pushed open the driver-side door and stepped out of the Cadillac. My car was in the same spot where I'd left it.

I reached back inside and pulled the trunk latch, walked to the rear of the car and lifted the lid. Inside was a briefcase. I laid it flat and popped it open. Inside were hundred-dollar bills, a handgun, and a bag of what I guessed was cocaine. There was also a needle and an orange strap. I picked up the bag and under it was a notebook. I opened it but had no idea what was written inside. All I could make of it was that whatever was written reminded me of something I'd seen in school. Formulas, perhaps.

I turned when I felt Annie walk up behind me.

"Is that yours?" she said, looking at the briefcase in the trunk.

"No. It must belong to those men. Or whoever it is they're involved with."

"What are you going to do with it?"

I looked around the parking lot. "I'm not going to leave it here, that's for sure." I closed the briefcase and took it from the trunk, slammed the lid closed, and walked toward my Jeep.

"Henry?" Annie said.

I turned to look at her, but she had stopped. "What's the matter?" I said.

"Maybe I should go," she said.

"Go where?"

"Back out West. I don't want to be involved in any of whatever's going on here. I'm not the kind of person who can handle the thought of having to sleep with one eye open."

"Not many people are," I said. "But I understand."

We continued toward my car. I popped open the trunk and slid the briefcase inside. I opened the passenger door for Annie and she stepped inside.

I backed out of the parking space and jumped onto San Jose Boulevard heading north. I took the ramp for 295 and remembered I had a backup phone in the glove box. "Excuse me," I said and reached for the phone. I plugged it into the charger and watched it, hoping it had enough juice to cycle on.

I looked down at the speedometer and realized I'd almost hit one hundred miles an hour. The last thing I needed was to be pulled over with whatever it was I had in the trunk.

But the phone buzzed and I looked at Annie. "Can you answer that?"

She picked it up and said hello, then turned to me with the phone up to her ear. "It's Alex!"

My heart stopped. I reached for the phone, but Annie leaned away from me and out of my reach. "What are you doing?" I said. "Let me talk to her." I slowed down to the speed limit and shifted into the right lane, then pulled off onto the shoulder and stopped.

Annie had her finger up, listening to the caller I'd hoped was Alex. But the expression on Annie's face dropped. She reached out and handed me the phone. "He wants to talk to you."

"He?" I said. "I thought you said it was... " I put the phone up to my ear. "Hello?"

A man's voice came through the phone. "I want my money."

I yelled into the phone. "What did you do with Alex?"

"You want to hear her voice again, you'll get me my money."

"I don't give a shit about any money. You can have it. You tell me where she is, or I swear to God I'll... "

"You'll do what? You're a tough guy, Walsh. Is that what you think you are?"

"Put her on the phone so I know she's all right."

"Nah," the man said. "You'll just have to trust me. She's okay. At least for now."

"You meet me and let her go; you'll get your money back."

"I don't believe you're in any position to negotiate, Mr. Walsh. But I can promise you, if you cross the line and try to pull anything, you won't see Miss Jepson again. And that pretty thing sitting in your car with you right now won't fair much better."

I looked in my rearview and all around the highway. But I didn't see a thing. "Tell me where to meet you," I said. But there was no response. "Hello?" I said. "Are you there?"

The caller had hung up.

I pulled back onto the highway and slammed down on the gas. I shifted lanes and looked from the rearview to the side-view mirrors, hoping to notice someone following.

At the last second, I yanked on the wheel and took Exit 105 North. I looked up in the rearview but still didn't see another car behind us.

"Where are we going?" Annie said. Her voice cracked with nerves.

I looked at her but didn't answer, drove to the Jacksonville Zoo and pulled into the parking lot. I slammed my hand on the steering wheel. "Shit!" I yelled. I looked at the screen of my phone. The call had come from Alex's phone. I dialed it back, and the man answered on the first ring. "Don't call again," he said. "Wait for my call, and I'll let you know where to meet."

"Tell me now!" I yelled. "Don't you want your goddamn money?"

The phone went quiet.

"You there?" I yelled. "You coward! Meet me like a man, face-to-face. And you'll get your money."

It was still quiet, but then the man laughed into the phone. "Listen, Walsh. Keep your cool, will you? Alex will be fine, as long as you do what I say. Oh, and don't you dare call your friends at the sheriff's office. That's a sure way to get your pretty friend killed."

Chapter 13

I STOPPED DOWNSTAIRS AT Billy's Place before going up to my office upstairs. Billy had his back to me and Annie but glanced at us over his shoulder and did a double take when he looked at me. "Jesus," he said. "What the hell happened?"

I touched the dried blood on my face. I hadn't yet had a chance to clean myself up. I kept my voice low and leaned closer to him on the bar. "Alex is in trouble."

Billy's eyes opened wide. "She's not upstairs?"

I shook my head. "No." I looked at Annie, then thought for a moment. "I haven't actually been up there. But... she's being held. It's a long story. But I have a briefcase with a lot of money in it. And if I don't get it back to the people it belongs to, it won't be good."

Billy wiped his hands on the towel over his shoulder, then tossed it somewhere behind the bar. He nodded toward Chloe, the only other person behind the bar. "I'll be back," he said to her. "Keep an eye on things." He came around to my side of the bar.

"I need your help," I said.

"Say the word."

We headed up the stairs to my office. I was somewhat hopeful when I opened the door that Alex would be at her desk, waiting for me.

But no such luck.

I told Billy what had happened, about the overdose and how we followed the Cadillac and got shot at and chased into Moe's Furniture Warehouse."

Moe's? Down toward Mandarin?" Billy said.

I nodded. Long story short, a couple of men grabbed me from the back room at gunpoint after Alex and I got split up. I thought maybe Alex got away, but apparently not."

Billy turned to Annie. "What about you? You were there?"

She shook her head. "A man grabbed me from outside the hotel where I'm staying." She closed her eyes, looked to be holding back tears. "He said Henry would be killed if I didn't go with him."

Billy and I glanced at each other.

"So they held me in an old abandoned building up in Georgia, and—"

"Georgia? They took you to Georgia?"

"Right over the line on the southeast side of the Okefeno-kee National Wildlife Refuge."

Billy scratched his head. "Are you going to tell me what this is all about?"

"Ted Parker. I was warned to stop investigating his death."

"So how do we save Alex?" Billy said.

I looked down at the phone in my hand. "I'm waiting for their call."

Billy walked to the window in my office and looked out toward the St. Johns River. "Don't you think it's time to get the sheriff's office involved?"

"Not unless I want to put her in more danger than she's already in."

Billy turned from the window. "Why's that?"

"They said not to call the cops."

Billy looked at Annie. "Are you okay? Can I get you something downstairs? A drink?"

Annie shrugged, then shook her head.

"We need to bring her somewhere safe," I said. "At least until we can get her on a flight."

"On a flight to where?" Billy said.

"I'm going back out to California," she said.

"I thought you were moving back here?" Billy shifted his eyes to mine. "Didn't you tell me she was..."

"Can you help me get her out of here? Bring her somewhere safe?"

"I'll bring her to my house. Nobody'll get to her there."

I turned to Annie and tried to take her hand, but she pulled it away. "Go with Billy. He's got dogs and guns and whatever else to make sure you'll be safe. Maybe you can find a flight. But I hope you'll wait until I get back there for you?"

"I can call Tim Green. He'll fly her away from here. I can't promise he can get you all the way out to California, but—"

"Malibu," Annie said.

"Malibu?" Billy repeated. "Is that where you're going?"

She nodded.

Billy walked to the door. "Let me go downstairs, just make sure Chloe will be all right while I'm gone. I'll be right back up; we can get out of here." He took one step down the stairs, then turned to me. "You sure you don't need my help with Alex?"

I shook my head. "Just take care of Annie. I'll worry about Alex."

Billy continued down the stairs and I turned to Annie. But she looked away, then stepped to the window and stared outside.

The sun had started to set.

"Do you want me to go with you?" I said.

She shook her head but kept her back to me and didn't answer. "I'm a big girl, Henry. I don't need you to babysit me anymore."

I walked toward her and put my hand on her shoulder. I tried to ease her toward me. "Babysit you?"

She finally turned and looked at me. Her eyes were filled with tears. "I know how much Alex means to you."

I shook my head, ready to deny whatever I could. But I'd only be telling a lie. "I spent a lot of years thinking about you," I said. "You left me, remember? I never asked for any of this. But then you show up out of nowhere. Was I supposed to—"

"Just stop talking," she said, her voice breaking through her tears. She walked over to the couch and sat down on the edge, her elbows rested on her thighs and her face down in her hands. "I don't know what the hell I was thinking," she said. "What a mistake this was."

"I didn't mean for any of this to happen," I said.

She looked up at me and cracked a smile through her tears. "You never mean for anything to happen. But it does. I should have known better than to expect anything else."

I walked over and sat next to her on the couch. I didn't touch her. And I didn't say a word. The two of us just sat there, quiet.

"You'll always have something you're chasing, Henry. You'll never be happy with what you have."

I turned to her and shook my head. "What? How could you..." I stood up from the couch. "You don't even know me anymore. You come back here after *how many* years? And then it's my fault when things fall apart?"

Chapter 14

I paced the floor in my office waiting for the phone to ring. The people who had Alex had yet to call, and I felt helpless. Useless.

But I couldn't sit tight any longer and decided to take a ride over to the tennis club where Tucker Dennison, Ted Parker's partner, was a member. I'd learned he played almost every night after work and thought I had nothing to lose while I waited for the call.

Sure enough, next to all the white or silver Mercedes and BMWs was Tucker's car. The only difference from the others was his license plate, which read CHEMCORE, the name of Ted and Tucker's company.

I leaned against the front of my Jeep and waited for Tucker to show up outside. I had trouble trying to focus, wondering why my phone had yet to ring. But in the meantime, my only hope was Tucker could have some answers that might help.

I spotted him when he walked out through the front door and under the lights along the walkway to the parking lot.

"How'd you do?" I said, but knew Tucker didn't recognize me under the artificial lights over the parking lot as I walked toward him.

He popped the lid on the trunk of his car and threw his duffel bag and tennis racket inside. "Excuse me? Are you talking to me?"

"Your game," I said. "Or your match... Whatever you call it in tennis. Did you win?"

He squinted his eyes and stared back at me. "Oh, it's you," he said, with a taste of disgust in his voice. "I don't have time for this." He stepped to the driver's side of his car, pulled on the handle, and opened the door.

The door was the only thing between us.

"You're all alone?" I said, and looked around the nearly empty parking lot. I had the notebook I took from the briefcase in my hand and placed it on the roof of the car.

Tucker held up his phone. "Back away from me, or I'll—"

"You'll what? Have I done something wrong?" I shook my head and smiled. "Not yet."

"I'm warning you... "

"Warning me about what? You'll send your goons after me again?"

"My 'goons'?"

I leaned hard into the door and pressed it against him. Although he appeared to be in good shape, he didn't seem to have much strength.

"I'm warning you!" He lifted his phone and with his other hand tapped the screen.

But I ripped it from his hand and tossed it onto the front seat of his car. I'd pressed the door with enough pressure, he couldn't turn to reach for the phone. "I just want to talk," I said. "And I want you to tell me the truth."

He turned and looked toward the tennis club he'd just walked out of. "Tell you the truth about what?" He looked around the parking lot. "There are cameras out here, you know."

"Let's start with what you know about your partner's death," I said.

"The only thing I know is what everyone else besides you already knows: Ted's death was a suicide. It was his own doing."

"And now Ted's friend—one of your investors—is also dead. Coincidentally, she just happened to be one person

Ted had a close relationship with. She was someone he could likely trust."

"She was obviously a cokehead," Tucker said. "People like her, who live with high stress and don't like the idea of slowing down..." He shrugged. "It happens. And I wasn't the least bit surprised."

"But you knew her well, too. Am I right? You're clearly not too broken up about her death."

"She was an investor. I wouldn't say I had a personal relationship with her. Although, I did appreciate the things she did for us, to help us get the company off the ground."

"Oh yeah?" I said. "How much did she invest?"

"That's private information."

I put a little more pressure on the door.

"Okay, okay!" he yelled. "She didn't invest as much as the others. But we had an agreement with her."

"Like what?"

"She'd helped us get the machines... the lab equipment. In exchange, she had the contract for the upkeep. There was a lot of profit in it for her."

I eased up the pressure on the door.

Tucker squeezed himself out from between it. He straightened out his shirt. "Are we done here?" He looked inside his car.

But I turned and leaned against the door. "I'll let you know when I'm done. How does that sound?" I stared him in the face, but he turned and looked the other way.

"I don't know what you want," he said. "But I don't want to be involved in whatever it is. As far as I'm concerned, my responsibility is to my company. Ted is gone. I've had to accept the fact I lost a friend and a business partner. But it's time to move forward."

"You know what?" I said. "I don't give a shit what you want. Because you are involved in something. And I'm going to find out what it is. But right now, my number one priority is finding my partner. And the person who has her is apparently very interested in stopping me from finding the truth behind what happened to Ted. Right now, getting her back, unharmed, is my only concern."

The expression on Tucker's face changed. "I... I'm sorry. I didn't know you—"

"You didn't know I *what*? You don't know anything about it? You don't know why anyone would want me to stop my investigation?" I let my arms down by my side and straightened up from his door. I stepped toward him and clenched my fists. My heart pounded in my chest, and I had to fight the urge to smack Tucker right in the mouth. I stood inches from him, face-to-face. "Are you going to stand there and look me in the eye, tell me you know nothing about what might've happened to my partner?"

He kept his eyes on mine and didn't flinch. After a pause, he shook his head. "That's the truth. I'm not a criminal, Mr. Walsh. I don't know what might've given you that indication." He swallowed and pulled his shirt collar from his neck. "I'm a graduate of MIT. I have a PhD in chemical engineering. I'm a successful businessman, and—"

"Anything else you want to brag about?" I said.

He narrowed his eyes. I could see a sudden burst of confidence come across his face. "What I'm trying to tell you, if you'd listen, is I've done nothing wrong."

"I don't believe just because you have a PhD, you can't be a criminal. In fact, some of the world's greatest criminals are highly educated." I stepped closer to Tucker. "And when you get defensive the way you do, I can't help but be somewhat suspicious."

I stepped away from him and grabbed the notebook I'd placed on the roof of his car. I handed it to him with a nod. "Here," I said. "Open it."

Tucker took it from my hand and opened the notebook. He turned so the streetlight was behind him and over his head. He flipped through the pages. "Where'd you get this?"

"Not important," I said.

He kept his gaze on me. "Yes, I think it is important. Tell me where you got this?"

"Why don't you tell me what all of this means."

Tucker's eyes went back down to the papers. "This is the formula Ted created when we were at MIT. We were all still honing our skills. We were still raw. Still learning." He held the notebook up. "This is what led us to start Chemcore." He, again, looked down at the notebook.

"The people who have my partner, Alex... this is what I believe they're after. I thought I had a briefcase full of cash. But this was buried inside it."

Tucker stared back at me. "What are you going to do with it?"

"I'm going to use it to save Alex."

"But if this gets into the wrong hands... "

"All I'm worried about right now is Alex."

Tucker stared back at me and looked around the parking lot. Most of the cars that were there when I first arrived had left. But I wondered what Tucker had going on in his mind. I could tell his wheels were turning, and he was either going to make a run for it or jump in his car.

I ripped the notebook from his hand and walked away. "I'll let you know how it goes."

Chapter 15

FEW INROADS AND TWENTY-SOMETHING hours without a wink of sleep led me to Detective Mike Stone.

"It's two thirty in the morning," he said when he answered my call. "This'd better be good."

"Alex is in trouble," I said.

I know I got his attention.

"She's been kidnapped. And I need your help."

"Christ, Henry." A muffled sound came over the phone, like Mike was rolling around in his sheets. "Where are you?" he said.

"I'm out in the street in front of a man's home who might be able to help. I thought about kicking in the door, but I'm not sure that would be my smartest move."

"You can't just go kicking in some guy's door. You think Alex is in there?"

"I don't know."

"Well then, what the hell are you doing outside this man's house?"

"Because he has connections to Ted Parker. And he knows something about a chemical formula that's been missing since—"

"Ted Parker?" Mike yelled into the phone. "Goddammit, Walsh. I told you to…" He sighed into the phone. "Just give me the address, will you? I'm not going to waste my time arguing with you over the phone."

··········

I don't think fifteen minutes had gone by before Mike pulled up on the street in front of LJ's house and parked behind my Jeep. "They warned me not to call the cops," I said.

"Glad I'm not the only one you refuse to listen to," Mike said. He reached for his holster and unsnapped the top. He removed his Glock and held it down by his side.

"What are you doing with that?" I said, my eyes on the gun.

"You're going to walk up to a man's door at three in the morning, hope he comes to the door with a cup of coffee?"

"But I'm not sure this guy knows anything yet."

Mike shook his head. "Then what the hell are we doing standing in the street in front of his house?"

"This guy is the only other person Tucker Dennison said would've been able to get his hands on the formula I found in that briefcase."

"I thought you said this guy LJ was one of his partners?"

"He was. But he left to go work with one of Chemcore's competitors. And he was the person at the hotel with Olivia Peckham, the morning before Ted Parker hit the pavement."

"And these people are all in the same business?"

I nodded. "For the most part."

Mike took a breath and leaned back against the front of my Jeep. "I'll probably regret telling you this, but I got word a few hours ago that cocaine wasn't the only thing that showed up on Olivia's toxicology report. There was fentanyl in her blood. And what you saw on her desk was barely cocaine. Seventy percent fentanyl."

"So it's confirmed? She was murdered?"

"I didn't say that." Mike pulled a cigarette from inside his coat pocket and stuck it in his mouth but didn't light it. "All right, I don't have all night." Mike started toward LJ's front door.

I followed him, but stopped to check my phone when it buzzed in my pocket. "Mike! Hold up," I said, my voice hushed. "This could be them."

He turned to me. "Who?"

"Whoever has Alex," I answered. "This is Henry."

The voice on the other end said, "What didn't you understand when I told you not to call the cops?" I looked ahead at Mike, then stopped and looked all around. I looked out toward the street, into the woods, and even up into the trees. "Where are you?" I said. "If you're watching us, then why don't you come out and show your face."

"Oh, you're being watched. But not by me personally."

Mike stared back at me, then started to look around himself. "What the... who's watching us? He pulled his Glock from his holster and held it by his side.

I turned and looked back at the road, then to the house. I looked it up and down and wondered if Mr. Hoover was behind it after all. I covered the transmitter on the phone and whispered to Mike, "He knows you're here."

"Who knows I'm here?" Mike had an expression on his face I had only seen once or twice, with somewhat of a snarl to his lip.

I put the phone up to my ear. "Now what?" I said.

"Now? You can start by telling your cop friend to get the hell out of there. Then you take those documents and go to Memorial Park."

"Don't you dare hurt Alex."

"You have twenty minutes. Tell your cop friend to get lost. And if he or any other cop shows up at the park, she's dead."

The call ended.

"What'd he say?" Mike said.

I looked around, hoping to spot whoever was watching us. "They're around here, somewhere, right now. Whoever it is knows I called you." I took a deep breath. "I'm supposed to meet them at Memorial Park in twenty minutes."

Mike started for the street. "Well, let's go!" He tucked the Glock back in his holster.

"Mike, you can't. They see you at the park, they'll hurt her. He made that clear."

"Bullshit!" he said. "I'm going. You think I'm going to leave it up to you to save her?" He had his keys in his hand and stepped into his car.

"Mike!" I said and grabbed the top of his door before he closed it shut. "You can't. Just stay here." I looked over the roof of his car toward LJ's house. "What if you go talk to LJ?" Mike turned his head and looked across toward the passenger window. He shook his head. "I can't knock on this guy's door right now. You haven't told me shit," he said.

"Mike, you show up at that park, and there's no guarantee they won't kill Alex."

He stared straight ahead at the windshield, one hand hung over the steering wheel. He turned to me. "You call me as soon as you know something. I won't go to the park, but I won't be far away, either." He turned the ignition, slapped his car into drive, and disappeared down the street without another word.

· · · · • · • · · ·

I made it to Memorial Park with a few minutes to spare and stood outside my Jeep. I'd tucked the briefcase with the money and documents under the seat.

My phone vibrated and I answered right away. "I'm here."

"I know you are. But we're going to have a change of plans. Just to make sure the cop stays out of our business."

"He's not here," I said. I jumped into the driver's seat and started the engine. "Where do you want me to go?" I knew I couldn't play games and put Alex in any more danger than she was already.

"Ramona Elementary?"

"You want me to meet you at an elementary school? It's fifteen minutes away," I said. I took off and turned onto Stockton Street, drove the pedal to the floor and headed for Route 10.

"Well, then, you'd better hurry. And when you get there, I want you to drive around back. Wait by your Jeep, and have the briefcase in your hand. You try anything funny, and I'll shoot her right there in front of you."

"You do anything to hurt her, I promise you I'll…" I looked at the screen. The caller had already hung up. I drove as fast as I could and moved my eyes from the rearview to the side-view mirrors to not only see if I was still being followed, but to make sure I didn't pass any cops looking to hand out a late-night ticket.

I jumped onto 10 West and drove another two and a half miles and took the exit for Ramona Boulevard. I continued west and passed the RaceWay gas station, then less than a half mile later turned into the school.

The building was dark inside, but there were orange-colored lights on the front. I turned my headlights off and drove slowly around to the back. I drove onto a basketball court and into the middle of a small playground, then shut off the engine and waited.

I didn't see anyone else around and didn't like the idea of being out in the open inside the Jeep. I glanced at my phone expecting it to ring. I spotted a car coming through the darkness from the opposite end of the school where I'd just pulled in. The red lights from the brakes illuminated the metal playground equipment behind it. It stopped. I couldn't see inside but could see it was an SUV.

My eyes adjusted somewhat to the darkness, but the SUV was parked far enough away I couldn't see who it was, when one of the doors opened. The interior lights did not turn on, and I had no way of knowing if Alex was in the vehicle or not.

I stepped from the Jeep and left the briefcase inside. I know I'd been asked to hold it in my hand, but I thought it would make it too easy. All they'd have to do is take one shot, grab it from my hand, and be done with it.

At the very least, if they didn't see it, they'd need me alive.

I squinted my eyes and was finally able to make out a figure walking toward me through the dark. And by the time they were close enough, it was easy to see it was a man. And he had a gun in his hand.

"Where's the briefcase?" the man said. Although I couldn't see him well, he was short and stocky. Maybe fat.

"Where's Alex?" I said.

"You give me the briefcase, and you'll get a chance to see the girl. You keep playing games, and you will wish you had remembered to say goodbye to her."

I took a couple of steps forward.

"Stay where you are!" the man yelled. His gun was pointed my way.

"I'm done playing games with you clowns. You want the briefcase, then you'll have to show me Alex. I didn't bring it with me, so if you want it bad enough, you'll have to prove to me she's all right."

The man laughed. "You've got balls, my friend. But that's not how this works. See, if I want to, I can shoot you dead. Then we'll simply kill your lady friend."

"But if you kill me, you won't know where I hid the brief-case."

Again, the man laughed. "He pointed his gun toward the Jeep. "It's under your seat. So take the goddamn briefcase out and throw it to me."

I stared back at him and hesitated a moment. I knew right then I didn't have a choice. I turned and stepped to the driver's side of my Jeep, reached under the seat, and pulled out the briefcase. I held it up. "You want it?"

"Bring it to me."

I tossed the briefcase and skidded it over the pavement. It stopped a few feet in front of the man's feet.

He bent over and picked it up, then turned to the SUV, and blew a high-pitched whistle with his fingers.

With the help of the moon, which had broken out from behind the clouds, I could see a tall man step out from the SUV. He opened the back door.

I thought I could see Alex but it was too dark. "Alex?" I started to walk toward her.

The man closest to me held his gun up toward me. "Hold it right there," he said. "Show a little patience, my friend."

"I'm not your friend," I said. I watched and still couldn't see if it was Alex. "Where is she?" I yelled.

Finally, I heard her voice. "Henry. I'm all right."

She walked out of the darkness with someone else holding her by the arm. He wasn't close but I could see it was a tall man. Then I noticed the Ronald Reagan mask. "I already saw your face," I said. "So I'm not sure why you're hiding behind that mask."

The tall man stayed back with Alex, closer to the SUV and far behind his shorter friend. Nobody said a word.

The man with the briefcase turned and walked toward the SUV. He stopped with his back to me, and his tall friend shined a flashlight inside the briefcase.

"Let her go!" I yelled.

But the man didn't let her go. He yelled to me, "You already made a mistake, Walsh. I don't believe I can trust you."

"I did exactly what you said!"

"No, you didn't. I told you not to get the cops involved. But you did. And now you're going to see what it means when someone doesn't keep their word."

He let Alex go, and she started to run toward me.

"Henry!" she yelled.

But before she made it more than ten steps, the tall one with the Reagan mask lifted a gun and fired a shot.

Alex's arms flew up in the air, and she stumbled down to the ground.

"Alex!" I ran to her and tried to cover her with my body.

Another shot was fired but it didn't come from the same direction. I looked and saw the shorter of the two men drop to the ground.

Another shot was fired, and the tall one jumped into the SUV. He left his friend for dead.

I held Alex's head in my lap. "Alex? Are you okay?" I looked into her eyes.

She opened her mouth to talk, but no words came out.

The SUV spun around and took off in the other direction when another shot was fired. The rear taillights exploded as the tires squealed. The SUV took off around the corner of the building and was gone.

I looked up at the roof and saw someone looking down at us from over the edge.

"Is it bad?" the person yelled.

It was Mike.

"I think it is, Mike." I looked down at Alex, but her eyes were closed. "Alex, can you hear me?" I didn't want to move her, but it was hard to tell in the dark where the bullet had hit her.

I looked across the area toward where the other man had been shot by Mike. The man still hadn't moved.

Chapter 16

I WAS ALONE IN one of the waiting areas at Memorial Hospital when Billy stepped off the elevator and hurried toward me.

"Is she okay?" he said.

I stood and looked down the hall. "She's in surgery. It's been over an hour."

"I got here as fast as I could."

I nodded, and looked down the hall toward the double automatic doors. I wasn't sure if that's where the doctor would walk through to tell me how she was, but I kept looking anyway. "Did Annie get off all right?"

Billy nodded. "She did. Flight left at eight forty."

I thought for a moment how strange it was hanging around with my ex-wife for a handful of days. "Better off she's gone," I said. "For her sake and for mine."

"You miss her?" Billy said, although I wasn't sure if he was joking.

I shook my head and looked toward the double doors once again. "You know, every time I get involved in something, I wonder if it's going to be the one I regret." I felt my eyes water up and turned from Billy and looked out the window. "She doesn't deserve this. And it's all my fault."

"How did Detective Stone end up there?"

"He followed me. Calling him in the first place was a mistake. But if it wasn't for him, Alex and I would have both been..." I didn't finish because I still wasn't sure how or if Alex would come out of this alive.

"You can't blame yourself for what happened," Billy said. "This is your job. And it's Alex's job. If you wanted something that wasn't dangerous, you could've been a bartender. Or stuck with a security job you hated. But don't sit there feeling sorry for yourself because of a decision you had to make." He let out a slight laugh. "My biggest decision is what kind of steaks I'm going to have on the menu, so I respect what you do, Henry. A lot of people do."

I smiled, my lips tight together. "Thanks. I guess."

"She'll be all right. She's tough. You know that."

The elevator door opened and Mike Stone walked off. He headed toward us and gave me a nod. "Any word?"

I shook my head. "Still waiting. Could be another hour. Maybe more."

Mike gave Billy a nod. "Good to see you, Billy." He turned and looked up at the surgical monitor. "That's the one who shot her: Enrique Pacheco."

"In surgery?" I said. "I thought he was dead?"

Mike shook his head. "A good thing he wasn't. Hopefully, he'll come out of this, ready to talk." He looked away, down the hall. "But Alex doesn't make it, I've got one in the chamber with his name on it." He started to walk away.

"You know this is all connected, Mike. Don't you?" I said.

He stopped in his tracks and turned, then walked toward me. He got right up in my face. "You want a trophy of some sort? Like it's some competition because you were right?" I could smell the coffee and cigarette on his breath.

"It's got nothing to do with competition," I said.

"If you knew when to quit," Mike said, "we wouldn't be here right now, praying Alex makes it out alive."

"And if you and your buddies at the sheriff's office weren't so quick to close the books when that man hit the pavement outside the hotel, then—"

Before I could finish, Mike grabbed me by the shirt and pushed me back into the seats behind me.

Billy tried to get in the middle of it but got knocked to the floor.

Two deputies who had just stepped off the elevator rushed toward me and Mike and pulled him off the top of me.

Billy jumped up and pulled me back. "Come on, Henry. Take it easy."

Mike pulled his sheriff's office jacket and straightened it out. He stared at me, red faced, then turned and again headed for the elevator. He pushed the button and waited with his back to us.

The two deputies hung back and turned to me. "Everything all right here, Walsh?"

I nodded. "Mike still loves me," I said. "He's just mad he can't have me."

Billy pulled me away. "Come on, let's go grab a coffee."

We walked past the nurses' station and I stopped. "Any chance I can get an update?" I said.

One of the nurse's stared up at me. "What is the patient's name again?"

"Jesus Christ," I snapped. "How many times do I have to give you her name?" I shook my head and turned to Billy. "Does anyone know what's going on around here?"

"Sir!" the nurse snapped. "You had better be careful, or I'll have to call security."

129

Billy stepped between me and the desk. "He's sorry," he said. "It's been a long night. And he's worried. I'm sure you can understand."

I looked at the woman. "I'm sorry," I said. And then I felt on the edge of tears.

The nurse tapped the computer keys and stared at the screen in front of her. "Let me go find out if there's been an update." She got up from her chair and walked down the hall, pressed the button for the double doors. They closed behind her.

"When was the last time you ate?" Billy said.

I shrugged. "No idea."

"Let's go get you something to eat before you take it out on someone else just trying to do their job."

The double doors opened, and the nurse walked through and came toward us. "I wish I could give you more, but she's still in surgery. The doctor's assistant did say it's possible she'll be in for at least another hour."

I tried not to raise my voice. "That's all she said?"

The nurse nodded. "I'm sorry. As soon as I know more, you'll be the first to know." She looked from me to Billy. "If you're going to leave, you can leave your phone number with me, and I'll call you once I have an update."

I shook my head. "I'm not going anywhere."

· · • • · • • · ·

I might have dozed off, but jumped from my chair when I felt a hand rest on my shoulder.

"Mr. Walsh?"

It was the doctor who had performed the surgery.

"Is she all right?" I said.

"She's in recovery. The surgery went as well as expected, but we won't know enough until she's awake. She's heavily sedated right now, and we'll likely keep her that way for a little while longer."

"Can I see her?"

"We want to give her some time in recovery, then I, or one of the nurses, will come get you. She's only been out for a few minutes, and I know you've been out here the whole time, but if you can just give her time to recover. Maybe another hour?" He looked around the waiting area. "Are you here all alone?"

I stretched my neck and felt pain from my brief nap in the chair. "I don't know." I looked around. "My friend was here, but I guess I fell asleep."

"Are you the only... Does she have any family here?"

"Just me. At least here in Jacksonville." I thought for a moment, unsure of how long I'd been asleep. "I'm going to call her parents. They're up in Virginia."

"Oh," the doctor said.

"I wanted to wait, make sure she was okay." I shrugged. "Maybe that wasn't the right thing to do."

The doctor nodded. "Okay, well, Alex had a punctured lung, and the bullet was lodged in one of her ribs. We had to repair her subclavian artery."

"What does that mean?" I said.

"Well, it feeds a major artery, and runs from her shoulder." He shifted his stance and tucked his hands into the pockets of his scrubs. "If she didn't get here when she did, there's a good chance she would have bled to death."

I swallowed so hard it almost hurt. "But she'll be okay?"

He nodded. "We'll keep a close eye on her for the next twenty-four to forty-eight hours. The timeline is critical." He paused. "There's a very slight chance with damage to the subclavian artery she could've lost her arm."

"What? Are you serious?" I said.

He stared back at me. "I'm confident she's just about out of the woods. But if anything changes, you'll be the first to know." The doctor turned and walked away.

The bell on the elevator rang. Billy stepped off and walked toward me. "What'd he say?" He handed me a cup of coffee.

I took the cup and sat down on the edge of the seat behind me. I stared straight ahead, almost in a daze. "It sounds like she's going to be all right."

Chapter 17

I WAS ON THE top step at L. J. Hoover's house when a woman came to the door with a cup of coffee in her hand. Her expression was hard to read, but I assumed the strange man who hadn't showered or shaved in days raised a question or two.

"Mrs. Hoover?" I said.

"Yes?"

"Is Mr. Hoover home?"

She looked me up and down. "Mr. Hoover?" She shook her head. "No, I'm afraid not." A look of suspicion covered her face. "Who are you?"

"My name's Henry. Henry Walsh. I'm a private investigator." I pulled a card from my wallet and handed it to her. "I'm investigating the death of Ted Parker."

"Ted Parker? What exactly are you investigating?"

I didn't exactly answer her. "I understand your husband has known Ted for quite a long time, so I thought maybe—"

"LJ doesn't live here. Not right now," she said.

I followed her gaze toward my Jeep, and said, "I'm sorry to bother you, then. But is it possible you'd know where I could find him?"

She shrugged, then looked down into her coffee. "You might want to try his girlfriend's place."

"His girlfriend?"

"He denies it, of course."

"Does she have a name?"

She nodded with a slight smirk on her face. "Olivia. Olivia Peckham."

I stared back at her, somewhat surprised but I guess not completely. "Mrs. Hoover, you're—"

"You can call me Vanessa."

"Oh, right. Okay, Vanessa, uh, you've apparently missed some news. Olivia Peckham is dead. She died of a... they claim it was a drug overdose."

Vanessa gasped and put both hands over her mouth. "Oh, dear God."

"She had a relationship with Ted Parker. I know that much. And I have to be honest with you, Mrs... Vanessa. I believe your husband was at the hotel with Olivia the morning before Ted Parker was killed."

"Should I be surprised?" She looked away for a moment, her eyes headed toward the street. "Is LJ all right?"

I raised my shoulders. "I can't answer that. I have no idea. But why wouldn't he be?"

She gave me the once-over, then stepped back from the door. "Would you like to come inside?"

I nodded and followed her through the doorway.

She closed the door behind her and headed down the hall. "I'm shocked about Olivia. I'm just surprised I hadn't heard about it from anyone."

"Who would have told you?" I said.

"I don't know." She continued toward the back of the house.

I followed behind her and glanced into a room with a couple of couches and a large fireplace with a painting over the top of it. I was sure I'd recognized it but had no idea from where.

We walked into the kitchen and Vanessa gestured toward the island in the center. "Have a seat, please." She walked to the stove and poured hot water into a cup and dropped two tea bags inside. "Would you like some tea? Or something else to drink?"

I sat down at the island and shook my head. "No, thank you. Not right now."

She sat down across from me and looked down into her cup, both hands wrapped around it.

"Would you mind if I asked about your husband and his relationship with Tucker Dennison and, of course, Ted?"

She rolled her eyes. "Tucker Dennison. That man's responsible for pushing LJ out of the company."

"Tucker pushed LJ out?" I said. "He made it sound like Ted and LJ had the problems."

"Of course he'd say that. Ted was in the middle, from what I know. He was the link in the chain that pulled them all together." She sipped her tea and gently placed it down in front of her, resting her chin in her hand. "He was such a smart man. A good man."

"Ted?" I said.

She nodded.

"But LJ left on his own terms, isn't that right?"

"He saw the business heading in the wrong direction. So did Ted. They didn't want to compete with the big players in the industry, but that's all Tucker wanted to do. Once he saw the problems grow with Tucker, he left to go work for another firm called Invector."

"Olivia's company," I said.

"Yes. I didn't think it was a good idea. For more reasons than one." She again looked into her cup. "I saw the change in LJ right away."

"But if he didn't want Chemcore to get too big, why would he go work for a larger company?"

"He just wanted a change," she said. "I didn't like the idea from the start."

"But then his company wanted to buy Chemcore. That doesn't quite add up."

She stared back at me for a moment before she spoke. "I can't answer all of the questions, Mr. Walsh. LJ was his own man. We'd stopped having meaningful discussions a long time ago, and that includes anything having to do with this one buying that one, and—"

"Then how did you know about his alleged relationship with Olivia?"

"I followed him. One time he went right to her house when he told me he had a meeting."

I thought for a moment. "How do you know it wasn't just business?"

She rolled her eyes at me. "Do I look that foolish?"

I looked back at her but didn't respond. "When was the last time you saw him?"

"LJ?" She nodded. "Right after Ted died. LJ and I went to the funeral together." She got up from the stool and walked to a drawer, pulled out a pad and wrote on it with a pencil. "Here's LJ's cell phone, if you don't already have it."

I took it from her and looked at the number she wrote for me. "What about Ted's wife?"

"Lynn? What about her?"

"I imagine you know her pretty well?"

Vanessa cracked a slight smile. "Lynn and I used to commiserate all the time while our husbands tried to get that business off the ground. It took over their lives, and there wasn't much room left for their significant others." She turned and looked out the back sliding glass door and into the yard.

"You're still friendly?"

She leaned against the island and toyed with the cup in front of her. "We don't talk like we used to. But I still consider her a good friend."

I looked down the hallway toward the door. "I appreciate you talking to me. I have to head over to Memorial... my partner's in the hospital."

"Oh, I'm sorry," she said. "I hope he's okay."

"She's a she," I said. "Alex." As soon as I said her name I felt a lump in my throat. "In fact, she's there because of this investigation."

"Do you mean... your investigation into Ted's death?"

I nodded and held up the paper with LJ's number on it. "Of course, I'll get to the bottom of what happened to Ted. But now it's personal. If anything happens to her... "

"I wish I could help you," she said. She shifted her eyes to the floor for a moment, then raised them and again looked out into the yard. "If Olivia Peckham is dead, then where could LJ be staying?"

"Can't you call him?"

She turned to me and shook her head. "We had some strong words after the funeral. He dropped me off. I told him I was going to be meeting with a lawyer. He didn't like that."

I looked around for pictures. "Do you have any kids?"

Vanessa seemed to roll her eyes. "Why do people ask that when a marriage falls apart? Like as long as you don't have kids, it's not a big deal?"

"I didn't mean it that way. I'm sorry, I just thought—"

"No, it's fine." She walked to the sink and faced the window behind it with her back to me.

"I'll get out of your way," I said.

She turned from the sink and followed me to the door.

I reached for the knob and opened the door.

I stepped outside and Vanessa poked her head out the door.

"Henry?"

I turned when I got to the bottom step and looked up at her.

She stepped out of the house. "Do you think LJ has anything to do with everything that's happened with Ted and your friend in the hospital?"

I hesitated to give her an answer. It wasn't like I had one. "I haven't met your husband. I don't know much about him. But Ted's brother—"

"Jack?" she said.

I nodded. "He's my client now." I rested my foot on the lower step in front of me. "I know you're friendly with Lynn Parker, but it sounds to me like you didn't know she had hired me to follow Ted?"

"Lynn did?" She shook her head. "I had no idea. She never mentioned a word of it."

"I was there the night he, well, fell from the balcony."

"You were there? All because Lynn hired you to follow him? And now, you don't believe it was suicide? Is that because you saw what happened?"

141

"I wish I had. But no, I didn't."

Chapter 18

I pulled the Jeep over to the side of the road and dialed the number Vanessa Hoover had given me.

LJ answered on the first ring. "L. J. Hoover."

"This is Henry Walsh. I have a feeling you already know who I am."

The line went quiet, other than background noise coming through the phone.

"You there?" I said.

"Yes? Can I help you with something?"

"You can answer my question," I said. "Do you know who I am?"

"I might."

"You might, huh?" I waited a moment but didn't see the conversation going anywhere without a little more help. "Let's just say I have something you may be looking for."

"I'm sorry? Can you just tell me what this call is about? I'm a busy man. I don't have much—"

"How about you meet me, and I'll explain," I said.

"I just told you, I don't have much time. I don't know what kind of game you're playing... Mr. Walsh, is it?"

"Well, I think it would be in your best interest to make some time. How about in an hour we meet at Friendship Fountain?"

LJ was quiet for a moment. "It'll have to be another time. I can meet later, in a few hours."

"I know you were at the hotel the morning before Ted's tragic death. And I know you were there with Olivia."

"How did you—"

"I'll tell you more in an hour. See you then."

I hung up with LJ and immediately dialed the phone for Memorial Hospital. I was hoping for a good update, and the nurse I spoke with told me she was doing better. "She's strong," she said.

"I know she is," I said, and hung up the phone. I pulled out of the parking space and my eyes started to tear. Lacking sleep and any semblance of food in my body, my emotions were too far out of whack.

I stopped off at Baker's Dozen for a coffee and a bagel sandwich, hoping it would at least be enough to get me through a meeting with LJ without losing my mind and doing something I'd later regret.

· · • • • • • · ·

I sat alone on the bench at Friendship Fountain and looked at my watch. LJ was late, although I thought I'd give him the benefit of the doubt, especially since at first he said he couldn't make it. But I knew I had his ear when I told him what I knew.

Finally, I spotted a man I believed was L. J. Hoover. He walked toward me, and seemed to know without question I was the man he was there to meet.

He stopped in front of me, stood, and looked down at me. He had his hands in his pockets and looked around the area like he was worried we were being watched.

I studied his hands for a moment, the way he held them in his pockets. "You all right?" I said. "You look a little nervous."

He gave me a nod with his chin but didn't look me in the eye. "I don't have much time."

I slid over to one side on the bench, then sipped what little was left of my cold coffee. "You want to sit?"

He shook his head. "Just get to the point of all this. Tell me what it is you want from me."

"Well," I said. "You can start by telling me what was going on with you and Olivia at the hotel. And I don't mean any extracurricular activity. Or extramarital activity, if you'd rather call it that."

"I'm sure you know what happened to her," he said, finally looking me in the eye.

"Of course. I found her. But I have a feeling you already know that." He wasn't about to sit down on the bench and made me uncomfortable the way he stood in front of me. I got up and stood to the side, facing him. "What I'd like to know is what you were doing at the hotel the same morning Ted just happened to come down from the balcony."

"We were there for work," he said. "I met with Olivia to discuss business."

"Just business, huh?" I stared back at him. "I'm not sure that's a story your wife's going to believe."

LJ shifted his eyes down to the ground, then raised them to mine. "You spoke to Vanessa?"

"Whether I did or not isn't important. What is important is that you come clean with me; tell me what was going on at that hotel, and why you'd all be there when it's not exactly an out-of-town location?"

LJ shrugged. "We use the rooms for meetings. Especially when they're slightly more informal."

"Well, I have a feeling you know more than you're willing to share with me. But my partner is in the hospital right now and it's directly related to Ted's death. And the fact you were at that hospital with Olivia—Jack Parker's ex-wife—has me wondering what your role is in all that's happened. Not only with Ted and Olivia, but with my partner."

LJ shook his head. "I have nothing to do with any of it. I swear. And I left the hotel that morning after I met with Olivia, and—"

"You can drop the act, you were there to meet with her," I said. I gave him a nod. "You do coke with her, too?"

"Cocaine?" LJ shook his head. "No."

"Then on top of everything, I happened to find a briefcase in the back of a Cadillac that followed me from Olivia's house. And inside it was a scientific formula. I'll be honest; it's way over my head, but from what I'm told, you'll know as much as anyone exactly what this formula is, and how it got in that briefcase."

LJ looked away. "I don't know what you're talking about."

"Tucker Dennison claims you do. He said you're the only person besides him who knew anything about it, and nobody else would even know the value of it."

LJ stared back at me, quiet for a moment.

"Tucker's a liar. Everybody knows that."

"Is he?" I pulled my sunglasses from the collar of my shirt, slipped them on over my eyes. "What I don't get is why this so-called formula is only in hard copy. Why wouldn't it be digitized? In a computer somewhere?"

LJ again looked off, then moved his eyes around the area like he was looking for someone or afraid of who was watching. "It's handwritten?" he said.

"So you know what I'm talking about?"

He took a moment, then nodded. "This is why Tucker pushed me out of the company."

"Is that what happened? Your wife seemed to think you left on your own to go work for the competition." I folded my arms across my chest. "So I would imagine there'd be something valuable for you if you happened to get your hands on this formula they might be after?"

LJ shook his head. "You think I'd do that to Ted?"

"He's dead," I said. "And if the only person to lose anything is Tucker, sounds to me maybe you'd have plenty to gain." I thought for a moment. "So, can you at least explain to me why such a valuable formula would be on one piece of paper? And it somehow disappeared until now?"

"Who said it was only on one piece of paper? Ted had it translated to an encrypted code, then broken into smaller parts on different storage networks. Nobody but Ted would know how to pull it together. So when he died... "

The formula died with him, at least until the hard copy suddenly reappeared?" I started to walk away from LJ but turned back to him. "Did Olivia know about the formula?"

LJ gazed back at me. "Ted trusted her as much as anyone."

"Then it's possible she was holding it for Ted, and whoever killed her took it from her?" I took another step away from LJ but turned one more time. "You were the one person connected, and close, to both Ted and Olivia. Yet, you're the only one who's still alive?"

Chapter 19

I WALKED DOWN THE hall of the hospital with flowers in my hand for Alex. But when I turned into her room, Mike Stone was seated in a chair at the side of Alex's bed.

"Are those for me?" he said, reaching toward me with his hand.

I didn't answer him, put the flowers on a table under the window, and walked around to the other side of Alex's bed. I put my hand on hers. "Are you doing all right?"

She didn't look great. Her eyes were narrowed with heavy bags under them. Her face was white and without much color.

I pushed out a smile. "You look good."

She rolled her eyes. "Don't lie, Henry. You know I don't." She cracked a slight smile. "But I guess I'm doing okay. It's better than being dead."

Mike stood up from the chair and gave me a nod from across the bed. "Henry, can I talk to you outside?" He put his hand down on Alex's hand. "Get some rest." He walked out of the room.

"I guess the detective wants to have a chat," I said to Alex. "I'll be right back." I followed Mike out the door and into the hall.

"Listen," he said, "I need you to come down to the station as soon as you can."

"What for?"

"The man who shot Alex didn't make it, and—"

"And you never got anything out of him? The man's dead, and now we have no way of knowing who he was working for."

"We?" Mike said. "There is no 'we.' This is a matter being handled by the sheriff's office. And, as I was saying, if you can come down and at least look at some photos, then maybe we can identify some of the others involved."

"You think I'm going to help you, then just sit around and wait for you to cut through all that red tape, while someone's out there who'll do whatever it takes to shut me up?"

"You don't want to find the people who did this to her?" Mike said.

"Of course I do, but—"

151

"Well, then, leave it to the sheriff's office. This isn't some kind of game, Walsh."

"Game? Is that what you think I do? Play games? I'm a goddamn licensed private investigator. You think that badge of yours is—"

"Jesus, Walsh. Just come down the station, and do what you can do to help. Why's everything gotta be an argument with you? You think I'm foolish enough to believe, even if you gave me your word you'd stay out of the way, you'd stop doing whatever the hell you wanted to? My only option would be to throw you behind bars. Probably be the best thing for you. But I'm warning you, you put Alex in harm's way like that again... "

"I'm not the one who shot the one man who could've led us to whoever's behind this."

Mike stepped toward me, got his mug right up in my face. "If I hadn't shot that man, you and Alex would've been lying there in the back of that schoolyard. Waiting for the coroner."

· · · • • • • • · ·

Alex turned her head on the pillow to look at me when I walked back into the room. "Why am I the one who keeps getting shot?"

I shrugged. "They always try to take out the tough ones first," I said with a smile I had to force.

She smiled, then winced and tried to move her body into a better position. "I'm glad you and Mike seem to be on the same team for once."

"I'm not sure I'd say we're on the same team. The guy gives me little respect. To think that'll ever change would be a mistake."

Alex stared back at me with a thin smile. "You need him on your side, Henry. We need him on our side. This Lone Ranger crap doesn't work anymore. And the more we try to work around the sheriff's office, the harder it gets for all of us.

"I don't know. I think things have worked all right so far."

She huffed out a laugh, but I don't think she found anything funny. "You're not the one who's been shot, Henry."

I sat in the chair Mike had left next to the bed. I was quiet for a couple of moments, my eyes looking toward the window. "I'm sure Mike wore you out with questions, but... is there anything you can tell me about the men who kept you captive? Were you able to somehow figure out where they might've held you? Any voices you might've recognized?"

"They barely spoke around me. Until we got to the back of that school, I hadn't heard a word from any of them. My head was covered the whole time, with a little TV in the room up loud, so I couldn't hear them talk."

"Do you know if you were in a house? Or an apartment? Did you go up a flight of stairs, or—"

"Slow down with the questions," she said. "I'm still on pain meds." She let out a gentle laugh. "It was a house. There was a garage, with an opener. They led me through a door, and I could hear someone clanging dishes, so it must've been a kitchen. The room they had me in was on the first floor, but I heard someone go upstairs when we first got there."

"And they had your face covered the entire time?"

"No, not when I was in the bedroom. Someone with a mask came in, took the hood off my head before he left."

Alex became quiet, closing her eyes.

"I should let you rest," I said.

But her eyes opened. "No. I'm fine. Really. My eyes just get heavy from the meds."

"What did the room look like? The one you were in?"

"I think it was a kid's room, or at least used to be. The walls were yellow. It was actually comforting, not the room I'd expect to be held in." She looked up at the ceiling, then turned her head and looked at me. "Where's Annie?"

"She's gone. Billy took her to the airport and she flew out to Malibu."

"Oh," is all Alex said.

We both looked at the TV for a couple of moments.

"So those three men, were they the only ones in that SUV with you?"

"I wasn't sure what kind of car it was, but I figured it was an SUV." She nodded. "But yes, just the three of them. The driver was the big guy. Wore a Reagan mask."

"That's the one who had me and Annie."

"He's the one who called you, from the SUV."

I got up from the chair and walked to the window, looking down over the parking lot. I thought for a moment, then turned back to Alex. "This is all about a formula Ted had created. I don't know how many hands it's gone through, but the morons who had me and Annie disappeared after we'd escaped, and left the Cadillac behind. The briefcase was in the trunk with this formula inside that Ted, Tucker, and their other original partner, L. J. Hoover, used to create Chemcore."

"Was it a disc? Or on a thumb drive?"

"It's literally a hard copy, handwritten in a notebook."

"So who had it?"

I sat back down in the chair. "Tucker Dennison claimed it was stolen."

"Did he say what it is?"

"If I understood chemistry, I could tell you. All I know is there are people who will kill to get their hands on it."

Alex gave me one of her looks. "Yeah, I found that out the hard way." She looked tired.

I got up from the chair. "I'll let you rest. I'm going to go see Mike."

Alex smiled. "Are you really? That's good to hear, Henry. I know he has a funny way of showing it, but he has a lot of respect for you. And I know you have the same amount of respect for him. You're both just too hard headed."

Chapter 20

JACK PARKER HAD LEFT me a message when I was in the hospital with Alex, and I called him back on my drive over to the sheriff's office to meet with Mike. Jack's message sounded urgent.

"I've been trying to reach you," he said as soon as he answered the phone. "I feel like you've left me in the dark, and—"

"Listen, Jack. I'm sorry. It's been a tough couple of days, and I was hoping we could meet. You might be able to help me tie up some loose ends I'm having trouble pulling together."

Jack was quiet on the other end. "Henry? Do you think Olivia had something to do with Ted's death?"

I hesitated to tell him too much because I still hadn't had a chance to wrap my head around who was and wasn't involved. And without Alex, I felt like I was running on one leg. "I don't want to say too much, but Olivia and Hoover were involved in something."

"That's actually why I'm calling you now," Jack said. "I got a call from LJ And he wanted to know what would make me hire a private investigator when everyone knows Ted's death was a suicide."

"He's hoping you'll get me off his back?" I said.

Jack went quiet again. "Hoover's a good guy, you know. He and Ted were close. So I just hope you're not seriously looking at him, like he—"

"Are you telling me how to do my job, Jack? Because I'm not going to pick and choose who I investigate based on your personal feelings."

"No, I'm not. I'm sorry. It's just..."

"Jack, I'm going to have to call you back. I just pulled into the parking lot at JSO headquarters."

"You're at the sheriff's office?"

I turned off the engine and stepped out of my Jeep. "I'll tell you one thing, Jack. But keep this quiet. The detective I'm meeting with knows your brother's death may not have been a suicide."

"Oh wow. Okay, that's good news, right?"

"It doesn't necessarily get us closer to finding who's responsible. But, yes, I'd say it's good to have someone on the inside who's willing to work with me."

· · · · · · · · · ·

Mike Stone was already waiting for me when I walked into JSO headquarters. I followed him back to one of the interview rooms with nothing inside but three chairs and a folding table. The chair I sat down on was bolted to the floor and had a handcuff bar welded to the top.

I looked around the room. "I didn't know I was being interrogated."

Mike shook his head and looked down at his hands on top of the table. "You're not. If you were, I'd read you your rights and cuff your wrist to that chair." He looked up at me and almost looked to crack a slight smile. He got up from his chair. "You want a drink?"

"Jack Daniels?"

"No, but I can get you a coffee if you want one."

"I'll pass," I said.

Mike opened a folder in front of him, pulled out a picture and turned it toward me. "You know this guy?"

I nodded without hesitation. "Tucker Dennison." I looked up at Mike. "Why?"

"The old man next door to Olivia Peckham's house—the one who gave you the key—said he'd been at the house a couple of times over the last week or so."

"He saw him?" I said.

Mike shook his head. "I think he saw the car. Said his wife took down the plate. We ran the plate, turns out it belongs to Tucker."

"Did you talk to him already?"

"Not yet. Wanted to talk to you first, see what else you know."

I said, "Well, the truth is I'm not quite sure what to make of him. They're all pointing fingers right now. Tucker and L. J. Hoover had a falling out, and apparently LJ was having an affair with Olivia, although LJ somewhat denied it."

Mike looked down in the folder. "Olivia Peckham looked to have close relationships with all three men."

"But not necessarily sexual in nature," I said. "I mean, with the exception of Hoover."

"And LJ denied knowing anything about the briefcase?"

"Yes. Tucker and LJ both denied knowing anything about it, and how that formula happened to show up after it'd been missing."

Mike closed the folder. "We believe the briefcase came from Olivia's house."

"And the men who took it? You find anything on that building out in Georgia?"

Mike nodded. "The bank owns it. Hasn't had another owner in five years. So must've just been an abandoned building they used. Maybe just the one time with you."

"And what about the van?" I said.

"Show me a white van, I'll show you twenty that look exactly like it."

I sat, quiet, for a moment. "I'm glad you finally believe Ted's death wasn't a suicide."

Mike took a moment before he spoke. He looked toward the closed door. "I didn't say that," he said. "But the truth is, I'm more focused on finding the guy who shot Alex. That son of a bitch shot her right there in front of us."

I nodded. "I want him as much as you do, Mike. But the truth is, you find him... you find whoever's behind what happened to Ted Parker. The whole reason she was abducted was because we were investigating Ted's death."

Mike stared straight at me. He narrowed his eyes. "You think you're so smart, Walsh. But did it ever cross your mind Parker jumped from that balcony because he was in something way over his head? There were no signs of a struggle. He had no markings like someone had thrown him off. We'd see them, you know. He stood up from the table. "Listen,

161

the whole reason I had you come down is because I know you're not going to stop trying to solve this case. The only way I'll get you out of my way is to lock you up until my job is finished. And I'm not going to do that. But it makes no sense for us to fight against each other any longer."

"Oh, great," I said. "So now you want to be friends?"

"Don't be an asshole, Walsh." He walked to the door and looked through the narrow pane of glass into the hall. "I just think if we're both willing to compromise, share whatever details we can with each other, maybe we can nail these bastards."

Chapter 21

JACK PARKER WAS SEATED with his back to me when I walked up to the bar at Billy's Place. Billy's bartender, Chloe, was on the other side and poured a Canadian Club and ginger ale in front of Jack.

Chloe looked up at me as I sat down and pushed the drink across to Jack. "Hi, Henry," she said. "Long time, no see."

I looked behind her and around the bar. "Where's Billy?"

"He went to see Alex," she said. "I think he thought you were there."

Jack sipped his drink and glanced at me. "I'm really sorry about what happened."

"Me too," I said.

Chloe put a glass of Jack Daniels down in front of me and walked away.

I held on to the glass and stared straight ahead. "So, Jack, when you first came to me, you said Ted might've been into something and maybe gotten in a little over his head. But you said you didn't know what it was."

Jack nodded. "I didn't."

"Didn't? Is that past tense?" I said. I turned to him.

"No, I still don't know." He sipped his drink. "I knew he was under a lot of pressure. His friendship with his partners seemed to have fallen apart, which is something he was always fearful of. I'd seen it happen so many times before. And there might've been added pressure on Ted to sell Chemcore."

"Pressure from who? Tucker Dennison?"

Jack stared at me for a moment before he answered. "Ted was never one to point fingers. Especially not when his friends were involved. But he hinted at it enough that I have a feeling Tucker was behind the push to cash in."

"But Ted refused to?" I said.

Jack sipped his drink and nodded. "Yeah."

"What about Olivia? What was her take on it?"

"I don't know. She and I hadn't spoken in months."

"And what about LJ?"

"What about him? He got pushed out of the business, as far as I know. Clearly, he must not have been happy about it." Jack held up his drink and looked at it from the side of the glass. "I don't even know why I ordered this." He made a face. "Too sweet." He finished what was left in the glass and pushed it across the bar. He waved for Chloe. "Can I get a Johnny Walker Black, please?"

Chloe reached for the bottle from the back of the bar, poured Jack a drink and placed it down in front of him. "Anything else?" she said, and her eyes darted between me and Jack.

"Put it on my tab," I said.

Jack gave me a nod and watched Chloe walk away. "I don't know much about Ted and LJ's relationship after LJ left Chemcore. I never really got into the details with Ted."

I thought for a moment, picked up my glass to take a sip but stopped. "I told you what Hoover's wife said, didn't I?"

"You mean that LJ was sleeping with Olivia?" He paused, like he was thinking. "Olivia was beautiful, had plenty of money, a lot of energy, and she got along with most people."

I stared at Jack and couldn't help but wonder if he still had feelings for Olivia. "So what happened with you two?"

"Me and Olivia?"

"If I only went by appearances, I'd say you looked good together. You're a good-looking guy. She was an attractive woman…"

He looked straight ahead and held the glass up to his mouth. "Everything is different on the outside." He sipped his drink.

I looked down the far end of the bar and watched a young couple laughing together, having drinks and fun. I thought to myself, *Everything is different on the outside.*

"So you and Olivia split up, but Ted stayed close with her? You don't normally hear that: someone keeps hanging around his brother's ex-wife."

Jack laughed. "Ted looked up to her, but more like a big sister. He had the brains, but he wasn't exactly a business person. Olivia tried to help him with that, get him to look at things through a different lens. She used to say maybe he was too nice."

"Enough where maybe one of his partners might've felt being nice wasn't good for business?" I said.

"You mean, to a point one of them would kill him?" He looked straight across the bar without answering.

"Do you think Ted was cheating on Lynn?"

Jack shot me a quick look and shook his head. "I don't think so, although I'm not sure he would have told me if he was. I'd say there were things about his personal life he may have chosen not to share with me. But, either way, their marriage wasn't going to last." Jack held his glass in front of him, his elbows on the bar. "You ask me, I wouldn't be surprised Lynn really believed he was cheating on her. She might've hired you just to cover her bases. Maybe get lucky he was cheating, make things easier in a divorce."

I nodded. "That thought did cross my mind. She was never even able to give me the name of any woman she suspected he might've been fooling around with."

Jack lifted his drink, tossed back whatever was left in the glass and slapped it down in front of him.

Billy walked through the swinging door from the kitchen, a somber look on his face. "Don't you have your phone?" he said.

I stared back at him and pulled my phone from my pocket. I'd missed six calls from him. "Shit, I'm sorry. I had the ringer turned down."

"It's Alex," he said. "She's not good."

I jumped up from my stool. "What? Why? What did they say?" I shook my head.

"Not much. At least not to me. Her parents were there. I heard the doctor tell them there's an infection. But I didn't want to bother them asking for details."

I nodded. "I talked to them this morning when they got in from Virginia. They'd talked to her. Alex was doing great."

Billy looked down at the bar for a moment, then looked up at me with moistened eyes. "I'm afraid it's not good."

I shook my head. "She's strong, Billy."

Jack sat there, watching us. "I'm so sorry," he said. "If there's anything I can do."

We both looked at him, but neither Billy nor I responded.

I headed for the door without another word to anyone and looked down at my phone, wishing I had gotten Billy's call the first time.

· · · · • • • · · ·

I walked onto Alex's floor at Memorial and hurried past the nurses' station, in case they weren't allowing non-family visitors. But nobody said a word, and I continued down the hall until I got to Alex's room.

The door was ajar and I pushed it open, stepped around the corner expecting to see Alex. But she wasn't there. In her place was a young man who looked up from his phone and stared back at me without a word.

I walked out and had to stop myself from running full speed but moved well beyond a normal pace until I got to the nurses' desk. "Where's Alex? Alex Jepson?"

The older woman behind the desk looked up from her computer as if she didn't hear a word I'd said. "Excuse me? May I help you?"

"Alex Jepson." I pointed toward her room. "Where is she?"

"Oh, Alex has been moved back into intensive care."

"Where? What floor?"

"The ICU? It's family members only, right now. Are you family?"

I didn't hesitate. "Yes, I am."

She nodded toward the elevator. "One floor up."

I turned and ran past the elevator and crashed through the door right after it, ran up a flight of stairs and pulled open the door. I stood in the hall and looked back and forth, saw a doctor step from one of the rooms. I ran toward him and grabbed his arm. "Alex Jepson," I said. "I'm looking for Alex Jepson."

He yanked his arm from my grasp. "Sir!" he said with a snap to his tone. "You'll need to go to the front desk if you need help." He turned, grabbed a folder from the plastic pocket next to the door, and opened the door to the next room. He disappeared inside.

I moved as fast as I could down the hall. All the rooms' doors were closed, and I continued until I got to the desk at the very end.

"Ma'am?" I said to a nurse, with her back to me, standing in front of a filing cabinet. "I'm looking for Alex Jepson. She was supposed to be moved up here."

A voice called from behind me. "Henry?"

I turned. Alex's mother stood behind me. She had tears in her eyes. Just behind her, in a chair in the waiting area, was an older man I recognized as Alex's father. He leaned forward with his elbows on his knees and looked up at me.

I hugged her mother. Her father stood and walked toward me, reached out, and shook my hand.

"Is she okay?" I said.

Neither answered but instead just looked at each other.

Her father said, "She's in surgery. She had a blood clot in her lung. It caused an infection, from what we were told."

"They're doing all they can," her mother said.

Her father looked down toward the floor. He lifted his eyes to mine, shaking his head. "I don't want my little girl to die," he said. He wiped a tear from his cheek with the back of his hand. "I need to know what happened."

Chapter 22

I JUMPED UP FROM my soaked sheets, startled. Sweat poured down my face. I wasn't sure I was fully asleep. Stuck somewhere in between my conscious thoughts and whatever else was boiling deep in my brain when I dozed off. The light next to my bed was still on.

I'd gotten used to it. That's how it'd been for a couple of years now. I didn't believe in taking prescription drugs to help me sleep, although I'd tried everything else.

A real sleep, a deep one, was as rare as a blue moon.

Until that point I hadn't been able to picture the face of the man who wore the Ronald Reagan mask until I knocked it off his face. All I could see, no matter how hard I tried, was the stupid mask. But somehow, in my dream, the image of a tattoo on his forearm, just above his wrist, finally came to me.

I jumped up and hurried into the kitchen, frantically pulling open drawers to find a pad. I'd taken to art as a kid but hadn't done much with it since, but started to sketch out the image I had in my head.

It may not have been much, but it was something.

I grabbed my phone. It was a little after midnight on the West Coast when I dialed Annie's cell phone.

She answered on the first ring. "Henry? What are you... Are you okay?"

"I don't know. Yeah, I guess. You okay out there?"

She was quiet for a moment. "I think I am, Henry. I'm going to stick it out."

"You need to be happy."

She didn't respond. "Are you sure everything's all right?" she said.

"Actually, no. Alex is in the hospital."

"Oh no! Why? What happened?"

"She was shot in the back. The same men who held us are responsible."

"I'm so sorry. I wish there was something I could do. Is she going to be all right?"

I hesitated to answer. Because I didn't have the answer. I could only hope.

"Last I knew she had surgery, and had gotten out when I left. She's in the ICU at Memorial." I had to close my eyes and take a deep breath or else... "Listen, there is something you can do."

"Anything."

"It's easy. I just need you to think. Remember the main guy? The one with the Reagan mask?"

"Of course I do."

"He had tattoos running up and down his arm."

"His whole body was covered, from what it looked like," she said.

"Well, I fell asleep and had a dream, right before I called you. I saw one of the tattoos. I don't even remember seeing it in person—I mean in real life, when we were there—other than just now in my dream. It's like my subconscious took a snapshot. I was able to draw it. I'll send it over to you so you can see it. If you take a look, and it looks like something you might've seen, then I'll know I'm not crazy."

"Can you send it to my phone?" she said.

I took a photo of my sketch, then sent it over to Annie in a text. "You should have it," I said.

"Hold on." The line went quiet for a couple of moments, then she came back on the line. "You drew this just from memory?" she said.

"No. Like I said, I don't remember seeing it. I dreamed about it."

"Well, you're right. He had this on his wrist. I do remember, but I would've never thought of it. He had so many up and down his arm." I could hear a TV or radio on in the background but Annie was quiet. "But do you know what it is?"

I looked over the drawing. "Well, no. Not yet. That's the part I'll have to figure out. But, I swear, I've seen it before. I can't imagine it'd just come to me like that, out of the blue."

"The brain can do funny things," she said. "Maybe somebody delivered a message to you."

"All right," I said. "We don't have to go that far. You and your newly found spirituality out there on the West Coast."

She laughed. "What? I'm serious. You never know how some things work."

We both stayed quiet.

"Henry?" she said. "Don't you think you should just bring your drawing to the sheriff's office? See what they can do with it?"

"I'm working directly with Mike Stone," I said. "He and Alex have been friends for a long time, so I have to trust him this time."

"They're friends?" she said. "Is that it?"

I thought for a moment. "I guess I'm not sure. I used to wonder if there was something more there."

Annie let out a slight laugh into the phone. "No wonder you don't like him."

"When did I tell you I didn't like him?"

She said, "You didn't have to say a word."

· · · · • · • · · ·

I tried to get another hour or two of sleep after having the feeling my body didn't want to be pushed any more than it had already been. But I tossed and turned until a hint of orange filled a piece of the sky.

The sun was on its way up.

I jumped in the shower, got out and called Billy, hoping he'd be awake.

"Is she okay?" he said as soon as he answered. "I thought you'd call me last night."

"I almost did. But I kept falling asleep, waking up every half hour or so. I'm heading over to the hospital around eight."

"So no word from anyone? Her parents?"

I poured myself a cup of coffee. "I called and spoke to a nurse. She was asleep, came out of surgery okay."

"Why don't you stop by on your way out?" he said. "I'll make some coffee."

· · • • • • • • · ·

Billy was out on his porch with a coffee in his hand when I walked up the stone walkway and handed him the paper I'd used to draw the tattoo. "This mean anything to you?" I said.

He took it from my hand and studied my drawing. He looked up from the paper. "Where'd you get this?"

"I drew it. It's the tattoo that was on the wrist of the man who held me and Annie. Same one who, I believe, shot Alex."

"You drew it from memory?"

"Yeah." I didn't need to go into how I pictured it in my dream. There was no need.

"And you think it's accurate enough?"

I shrugged. "I sent it to Annie; she recognized it right away."

Billy sipped his coffee and looked at the drawing for another few moments. "What makes you think I would know what it's supposed to mean?"

"I don't know. You have a tattoo."

He made a face and stared back at me. "Or is it because I'm of Chinese descent, and you think I would know what symbol you're guessing might have some Asian meaning?" He laughed and shook his head. "Is that it?" He stood up from his seat. "Chloe or Jake might know something about it," he said.

Chloe and Jake both worked for Billy at the restaurant, Jake being one with tattoos running up and down both arms.

Billy looked at his watch. "Jake's in there now, doing prep work. Why don't you follow me over, see what he thinks?"

· · · ● · ● · · · ·

Jake was outside the back door at the restaurant checking in deliveries from the seafood delivery truck. He lifted his eyes off the clipboard he held in front of him and gave me a nod. "Hey, Henry."

Billy stopped the man with the hand truck and lifted the cover on one of the fish buckets. He reached inside and pulled out a fish, gave it a sniff, and nodded at the man. "Looks good," he said. He placed the fish back inside the container and closed the plastic cover. He wiped his hands on his pants and took the clipboard from Jake. "Henry needs your help with something." He grabbed Jake's hand and lifted it up in front of me. "See?"

I was well aware of Jake's tattoos, but I'd never taken the time to actually study them. He had crosses and snakes and letters and flowers; you name it, Jake seemed to have it tattooed on his arm.

"What's up?" Jake said. He pulled his arm back from Billy.

I handed him the paper with the symbol I'd drawn on it. "Have you ever seen a tattoo like this before?"

Jake grabbed the paper from me and looked down at the drawing. "Where'd you see this?"

"On the arm of one of the men who put Alex in the hospital."

Jake looked at the paper again, then lifted his eyes to mine. "It's a prison tattoo. Only reason I recognize it is my guy—"

"Your guy?" I said.

"Yeah, the tattoo artist I use. He spent a couple of years in Raiford. A lot of his customers are ex-cons." He laughed. "I know that sounds funny. And if they're not ex-cons, most of his customers were recommended by someone who was."

"How'd you find this guy?" I said, out of curiosity.

Jake shrugged. "He's got a good reputation. Probably one of the best in Jax."

Billy looked up from the clipboard at me and shrugged. "Told you he'd know something."

"Jake, you sure you recognize this?"

He nodded. "Yeah, it's a whole group in there. I remember him telling me. I don't know if they're technically a gang or anything. But if you have that tattoo... You've spent time in Raiford."

Chapter 23

LYNN PARKER OPENED HER front door wearing a kimono over her bathing suit and a martini glass in her hand. She leaned on the knob with one hand, lifted the glass to her mouth, and looked me up and down. Her eyes appeared heavier than I remembered, her lids halfway down over her dark brown eyes. "Henry Walsh," she said. "I was wondering when you were going to come by to see me." Her words were somewhat slurred. "I've heard the rumors you're still trying to prove Teddy didn't take his own life?" She let out a slight laugh.

"I don't know what's funny," I said. "But my partner, right now, is in the hospital fighting for her life."

Lynn straightened herself up. The expression on her face changed. "I'm sorry. Won't you come inside?" She stepped back from the door.

I followed her inside, and we walked down a hall, through the kitchen at the back of the house, and out through a set of double doors and into the yard.

We walked out onto her stone patio to a small round table.

"Please have a seat," she said. "What would you like to drink?"

I wasn't usually one to turn one down, but it was still a little early. "I'm all right for now."

She flapped her hand through the air at me. "Nonsense." She looked at her martini glass, drank what was left, and started for the cabana next to the pool. "I'll get you something to sip while I get myself a refill."

She walked into the cabana and came out a moment later with a glass in each hand. "I hope you like Maker's Mark? It's what Teddy used to drink." She put the glass down in front of me.

The woman had clearly spent her morning with the bottle. She sat down and pushed open her kimono, shot me a glance some might consider seductive. If you'd asked me, I would've said she'd had enough to drink, just by looking at her heavy eyelids. She sipped her martini and kept her eyes on me from over the rim of her glass.

"I wanted to talk to you a little more about Ted's death. And see if you can perhaps help me with some of the things

I've discovered." I put my hand on my glass and had yet to take a sip.

She shrugged, eased her glass down on top of the table, and leaned with her elbows down, her hands together under her chin. "Whatever I can do to help you, Henry." Again, she gave me that look.

Maybe another time. Another life. She was beautiful; there was no doubt about that. But not for me.

"Okay, I'd like you to be straight with me, Lynn. Did you really believe Ted was cheating on you? Or did you hire me hoping I'd find something else?"

She leaned back in her chair and crossed one bare leg over the other. With her eyes down, she pulled the front of her kimono over her thighs. After a pause, she lifted her eyes and looked across the table. "Are you going to tell me about some crazy theory you have about why I'd hire a private investigator to follow my husband but not tell him the real reason why?"

I kept my gaze on her. I had a feeling the drinks she'd had would let her slide into saying something she'd regret.

"Would you like me to confess? That I went to that hotel, slipped past your car, and threw him off the balcony myself?" She took a breath and rolled her eyes, then turned and looked across the yard.

"I just want the truth," I said. "I want to know the real reason you hired me."

She had her head turned, her eyes somewhere else. "Why does it matter to you?" She looked at me, gave me a nod with her chin. "You got your money. I paid you well."

"This has nothing to do with money. Alex is in the hospital. And nobody will guarantee she's out of the woods. And it's all because of whatever the hell happened that night at the hotel."

"I told you, I'm sorry about Alex," Lynn said.

"My point is, I know you invested your family's money to help them get Chemcore off the ground. So, to me, I can't help but think you had something to lose if the business fell apart. Or, on the other hand, you'd have plenty to gain if Chemcore was sold for as much as Tucker Dennison was hoping to sell it for."

"I didn't kill my husband," she said. "And you have some nerve trying to—"

"I'm trying to get to the truth. There's nothing more to it."

"Well, I wish you'd get it out of your head I have something to hide from you. You want to get to the bottom of what was going on at Chemcore? I'm not the person you need to talk to."

"I've already spoken to Tucker Dennison. I'm still trying to understand exactly why Tucker pushed LJ out of the business."

Lynn had a funny look on her face. "Is that what LJ told you?" She shook her head. "The truth is, Ted was the one who didn't trust LJ. He was the brains behind Chemcore. LJ's a smart man, but doesn't come close to having what Ted had upstairs. Ted was a genius. A scientist. He was never driven by money the way LJ and Tucker are."

"But doesn't that have something to do with not having to worry about money? I mean, he was married to you. And I understand money's never been an issue for you or your family."

Lynn shifted in her chair. "I won't deny the fact I had the money to support us while Ted tried to get his dream off the ground. But Tucker and LJ didn't have that. We never had kids. But they had mouths to feed at home."

We both sat quiet for a moment.

"This may be an odd question, but is there any chance you know anyone who spent time in Florida State Prison?"

She had a surprised look on her face. "Me? Well, I mean... I know lots of people. I've been in Florida my entire life. And they're not all good people." She finished what was in her glass, got up from her chair, and walked into the cabana.

She came out a moment later with her glass filled, two olives inside. "Like my mother used to say to me; you're driving me to drink. I can't be sure if you're asking for my help, or if you're pointing the finger at me."

I reached for the glass in front of me and tipped my head back. I threw the whole thing down my throat and got up from the chair. "Lynn, I'm asking everyone. And I'm pointing the finger at everyone. Until I get to the truth, I have no other option."

Chapter 24

THE MORE THE DAYS passed without Alex by my side, the more I realized how much weight she carried on her back. I missed her. And it wasn't just about work.

Her health had improved, and when I stopped by to see her, she was sitting up in bed. Her parents were in the room, seated in chairs near the window, their eyes up on the TV.

I leaned over and kissed Alex on the forehead. "You look better."

She smiled, and her eyes went to her parents.

They both looked exhausted, like they'd aged ten years since they first arrived from Virginia. "Have either of you slept?" I said. "I'll stay with her if you want to go back to the hotel and get some sleep."

Alex lifted her head from the pillow. "Mom. Dad. You don't have to stay here. I'm feeling better. You're going to get sick yourselves, if you don't get some rest."

I had my hand on the rail next to Alex's head, and she put her hand on top of it. "I'm sure Henry will let you know if I need anything. He'll take care of me." She smiled, but then her expression changed. "I miss Raz."

Her dog, Raz, spent some time at Alex's neighbor's house. But he was also under group care and even spent time with Billy.

I nodded. "Raz misses you, too."

Her parents stood next to me, then each leaned down and gave her a kiss before they turned for the door.

"We'll be back in a couple of hours," her mother said.

Alex watched them both leave the room. Her eyes filled with tears. She wiped her cheek with her hand and closed her eyes for a couple of moments. She reached for the remote on the table next to her and turned off the TV. She turned and stared at me. "You look like shit, you know."

"Oh, thank you," I said.

"No, I mean it. You look tired. And you smell like you've been drinking. It's a little early for that, isn't it?"

"I went to see Lynn Parker. She was already a couple of martinis into the morning, and forced me to have a drink with her."

"Oh, I'm sure she really had to twist your arm?"

I ignored her questions and pulled the folded piece of paper from my pocket. "You recognize this?"

She took the paper and looked it over. "What is it?"

"It's the tattoo on the arm of the man who held me and Annie. The same man who pulled the trigger."

She had a confused look on her face. "You saw this on his arm?"

"I had a dream about it. I swear I don't remember seeing it. But Annie did, as soon as I showed her what I'd drawn."

"You're talking about the tall one with the Reagan mask, right?" she said.

"Yes, and they had the same masks when they held me and Annie. The shorter one is dead. He's the one Mike shot from the rooftop."

She stared at the drawing, then shifted her eyes to mine. "It's all so blurry. I barely remember being back there."

I put my hand on top of hers, then looked toward the door just to make sure her father, by some chance, wasn't still standing there. "Your dad was pretty upset," I said. "I don't think he wants you involved in this shit anymore. And I can't say I blame him. It just seems to—"

"Henry, he was a cop for forty-three years. He has no right to say anything."

I stared into her eyes, then shook my head. "You're his little girl, Alex. No matter what. And no man wants to see his little girl shot not once, but twice in the same couple of years."

I pulled a chair over and sat down next to Alex's bed. My head had started to feel heavy. My vision was blurry, and I rubbed both eyes trying to clear the fog.

"Are you okay?" Alex said. She pushed herself up in the bed.

I took a deep breath and nodded. "I think I just need something to drink. I'm a little dizzy."

"Why don't you go get some food? Get yourself a drink. I don't care if you were forced or not, it's pretty foolish of you to start drinking early in the morning."

"I swear, I wasn't going to touch it. She pushed it in front of me. Right before I left, I threw it back. You know I hate to waste a good drink."

I started to stand from the chair but fell back down. The room had started to spin.

"Henry?" Alex reached for me from her bed.

I had my head down in my hands, my elbows down on my knees.

"Henry?" she said again. "Are you okay?"

I looked up at her and shook my head. "No, I don't think I am."

All I could taste was the booze. "I feel like I've been poisoned." And then it hit me. "That drink. She... she put something in my drink." Before I got another word out, everything turned black. I felt myself fall from the chair. I hit the floor, but that was all I remembered.

· · · • • • • · · ·

I woke up in a small room in the hospital, lying on top of a gurney. Curtains were pulled all around me. My head pounded with each beep from the machine next to my bed, the wires from it taped to my chest. It hurt to open my eyes. I had a needle in my arm attached to a thin tube up to the IV hanging on a hook over my head. My throat burned. The pain in my stomach was almost unbearable.

The curtain was opened, and a young doctor, or maybe a nurse—I had no idea—stood at the foot of my bed. "Good to see you awake," he said.

"What the hell's going on?" I said. I grabbed my throat with my hand. "Can I get a drink?"

The young man nodded. "We pumped your stomach. You were poisoned. Your friend upstairs, Alex Jepson, said you told her you'd had an early morning cocktail. If that's all you had, then it's likely that was the source of the toxins we detected in your urine."

I stared at him, still in disbelief. "It was Maker's Mark."

He nodded. "You're lucky you were here in the hospital. It could have killed you if you weren't."

· · · · •· • · · ·

The doctors had wanted me to stay overnight for observation, but there was little chance I'd let them do that. So I went up to see Alex hoping they'd have the results of whatever it was Lynn must have slipped in my drink.

"Why would she poison you?" Alex said. She was sitting up in bed and looked a lot better than how I felt.

"It doesn't make any sense at all," I said. "I mean, she was our client. She knew I was there watching Ted. For her to try to kill me to stop me from getting to the bottom of his death?"

"What if she knows who killed Ted?" Alex said. "And she's trying to protect whoever it was?"

I nodded. "I thought about that."

We were both quiet, and neither had an answer.

"You need to call Mike," she said.

"I was planning on it." I leaned over and kissed her forehead. "You okay if I leave?"

Alex smiled with a nod. "Of course I am." She gazed into my eyes. "But are you okay?"

"Don't worry about me," I said. "Get better. I know your father would rather have you give it up, but I'm working without thumbs when you're not around."

"Without thumbs?" She smiled.

"Whatever you want to call it. I need you back on your feet."

· · · • • • • · · ·

I called Mike Stone as soon as I left the parking lot at Memorial.

"What the hell happened to you?" he said. "We just got word from the hospital you were a victim of poisoning?"

"Yes, turns out that's a fact. That's why I'm calling."

"I'm on my way there right now," Mike said.

"To where? The hospital?"

"Yes. They said they'd have the results of whatever it was you ingested."

"Well, I don't know what it was. But Lynn Parker slipped it in my drink."

"Your drink? From last night?"

I hesitated a moment. "No, this morning."

"Jesus, Walsh. You drink in the morning? That's a problem in itself, don't you think?"

"It's not the point," I said. I didn't need anyone, especially Mike, to lecture me.

"Why don't you wait for me at the hospital," he said.

"I already left. I'm going back to Lynn Parker's."

"Christ, no. You have to wait. You gotta do this the right way. If she intentionally poisoned you as you're saying, then you can't just go over there, start throwing around accusations. You'll blow the whole goddamn thing up." He shook his head. "You're acting like these young officers I have to deal with all the time. You should know better."

·········

Mike Stone leaned against his Crown Victoria, smoking a cigarette when I pulled up next to him at the back of the parking lot at Memorial Hospital. He looked at his watch. "Where have you been? I told you ten minutes." He reached into his car and pulled out a folder.

I stepped out of the Jeep.

"Here," he said, handing me the folder. "Fentanyl."

It was the paperwork from the toxicology report. "That's what killed Olivia Peckham," I said.

"You think I don't know that?" Mike said. He took a deep drag of his cigarette, then dropped it on the ground. He crushed it with the front of his shoe, then leaned over, and picked it up.

"So if Lynn Parker's the one who poisoned me—"

"She killed Olivia Peckham," Mike said. He pulled another cigarette from his pack and stuck it in his mouth. He cupped his hand around the end and lit it with his Zippo. He took a drag, then exhaled in front of my face. "I want you to stay out of this," he said.

"Stay out of what? Are you kidding me?"

"I told you, we're going to do this the right way. We get a search warrant, follow the rules, and if we can prove it was Lynn Parker, we'll nail her right then and there."

I said, "But here's what doesn't make sense. If she had anything to do with Ted's death, or even Olivia's, then why the hell would she hire me in the first place? It makes no sense."

Mike took another drag from his cigarette. "I still haven't seen any real proof Ted Parker's death was anything more than a suicide." He reached for the handle on the driver's side of his Crown Victoria and pulled open the door.

I put my hand against the door and prevented Mike from opening it.

He knocked my arm out of the way. "What the hell do you think you're doing?"

"How can you still believe Ted Parker jumped from that hotel? You have to be a moron not to believe somebody killed him?"

"What I believe and what the evidence proves are two different things, Walsh. You don't have to worry about things like evidence, because you can just fly around by the seat of your pants." He scratched his head, the cigarette stuck between his fingers. "I don't know how many times I have to tell you this: I'm more interested right now in finding the man who shot Alex. If you can't understand that, then—"

"Why does it have to be one or the other?" I said. "I'm telling you right now, they are one hundred percent connected. I just don't know why you don't care about the truth."

Mike laughed. "You always make it sound like you're the only one interested in finding the truth. What the hell do you think I do each and every day of my life?" He shook his head. "The thing is, Walsh, sometimes you gotta make choices." He pulled open the driver's side door and stepped inside. He pulled it closed, started the engine, and rolled down the window. "Just do me a favor. Stay out of the way, will you? Let me do my job. I need anything from you, you'll be the first to know." He slapped the shifter on the steering column and backed up out of the parking space, drove across the back of the parking lot, and disappeared into the sea of parked cars.

Chapter 25

I SAT AT THE bar at Billy's Place with a glass of soda water with a lime, in front of me. It wasn't often you'd see me at any bar without a bottle of beer or a whiskey. But I knew my carelessness had finally gotten the best of me.

Of course, I wasn't about to blame booze. But the point was, I'd thrown back a shot of bourbon at a time of day I normally didn't drink. And it almost killed me.

Billy grabbed my glass and topped it off with more soda from the gun behind the bar. He leaned on the bar, his hands spread wide from his shoulders. "So you're really not going to do anything? I don't believe it."

I took a sip of soda and leaned against the back of the stool. "I'll see how long I can sit on the sidelines. The problem with law enforcement is there are a lot of rules officials need to follow. To me, it just makes it harder to get things done. I mean, I don't mind rules, but—"

Billy laughed. "You don't mind rules? Tell me another one."

"If you'd let me finish. What I was going to say is I understand the need for rules. But when you know something needs to happen, but it's held up because of red tape or bureaucracies, questions don't get answered fast enough. And when you lose time... "

"Mike told you to stay away from Lynn Parker's house. He didn't tell you to stop investigating entirely, did he?"

I shook my head. "No. Because he can't."

I knew I had to get to the bottom of what'd happened to Ted if we were going to find the person who shot Alex. And in my mind, I started to question every single person I'd come across ever since Ted fell from that balcony.

"You know," I said, "if Lynn Parker could've had something to do with it and she was my client, then maybe I need to look at Ted's brother, Jack, too. I have no idea what the ulterior motive would be for Jack to hire me if he was behind anything that's happened. But I don't think I can rule anybody out." I finished my drink and got up from the stool. "I'm heading up to my office."

"Raz is up there. Chloe said she'd take him for a walk when she gets back."

"Thanks. Maybe I'll take him for a walk. I could use some fresh air, do some thinking. I have a feeling if Raz could talk, he'd make a good partner."

....

It was almost midnight, and I'd been at my desk for more than a few hours going through the video we copied from the hotel. I was sure I'd watched every second of it already, but it didn't hurt to go through it one more time. I was tired at the point I couldn't look at the footage any longer. I watched at double speed and saw very few people come and go the night I was there to watch Ted.

But I stopped on the same pizza delivery person who stood near the elevator that Alex and I had noticed the first time we watched the video. He wasn't a young kid, although it was hard to see the face with a hat pulled down low over his eyes. The metal, gold-rimmed glasses reflected the light from the ceiling over where he stood.

The elevator door opened and the man disappeared inside. Nobody else stepped off the elevator. And for the next few minutes of footage, nobody else got on.

Alex would have been able to zoom in on the man, but I wasn't exactly sure how to use the software she'd installed on one of the computers.

I slowed the video down to normal speed when I saw myself walking into the hotel lobby from outside. I watched myself on camera run toward the back. It was at that point Ted Parker had hit the pavement by the pool.

The elevator was still in view. Three minutes and twenty seconds had passed from the moment I walked off camera and ran toward the back of the lobby. It was then the pizza delivery person stepped off the elevator. He held a pizza box in his hands.

I wish I'd known how to use the damn video software. If Alex were only here to help. But she wasn't.

So I sent her a brief text:

You awake?

She replied right back:

Impossible to sleep here.

My phone rang a moment later. It was Alex.

"You all right?" she said.

"Me? Yeah, I think so. I was afraid to text you. It's late."

"I'm just lying here, listening to the beeps," she said. "And I barely know what day it is. Never mind what time it is."

The line went quiet.

"So what's up?" she said. "I assume you weren't just sending me a text for the hell of it?"

I laughed. "I'm at the office, looking at the video footage from the hotel."

"You see something?" she said.

"Maybe. A pizza guy stepped on the elevator ten minutes before Ted hit the ground outside that hotel. Then I saw the same person step off. I'd already gone out toward the pool at that point. And the guy had the pizza box in his hand. The way he's carrying it, it's almost as if the box is empty."

"Can you see the face?" Alex said.

"No. I was hoping you'd be able to help with that. I have no idea how to use this software."

"To do what? Zoom in?"

"Yes, exactly."

"Just hold down the control key and the plus sign."

I put the phone down on my desk and put it on speaker. I zoomed in and saw the image on the box. "A place called Dino's Pizza."

"I've never heard of it," she said. "Did you zoom in on the man's face?"

"He's not looking at the camera. He knows it's there." I backed up the footage and watched it again. "Nothing."

"If it can wait until tomorrow, I'm being released in the morning."

"You are?" I couldn't have been happier to hear the news. "I'll come get you, if you want? Unless your parents are going to drive you back?"

"You can come here if you don't mind. I can call you when I know what time it'll be. But if you can't... they'll drive me home."

"I'll come at eight. Hopefully, they'll let you out first thing."

"It could be later. The nurse didn't know."

"That's okay," I said. "I'll see you in the morning. Maybe you should get some sleep."

"I was just going to tell you the same thing."

Alex hung up, and I spent another half hour looking at the footage, playing around with the zoom on the computer. And I was able to get a fairly clear image of the floor where the pizza guy had stopped off on the elevator.

And sure enough, the light stopped on the seventh floor.

I looked up the listing for Dino's Pizza and found one down Southside. But the place online showed it was permanently closed.

Out of business.

· · · · •·•· · ·

I pulled into the parking lot and parked next to a white brick building with an old sign on the front I couldn't read. The windows were taped over and covered with newspaper. The parking lot was overgrown with weeds poking up through the cracks in the concrete.

I stepped out of the Jeep and walked to the building. It looked completely abandoned. But when I leaned in closer to the window, I could see a streak of light coming through from the inside. I turned my ear toward the window and heard someone inside. I walked around back and spotted a pickup truck with a Dino's delivery sign on top. I felt the hood. It was cold.

I looked around at the other buildings and didn't see many other cars around until something caught my eye: a white van, parked a few buildings down from what used to be Dino's Pizza.

Around the back of the building a heavy steel door was slightly ajar. I pulled on it, and dim light escaped from inside.

A voice called out. "Who the hell's out there?"

A man stepped around from the other side of a wall and saw me standing there, just outside the door.

"Someone's out there!" he yelled. "Get the sonofabitch!"

203

A shot was fired and I ran for my Jeep. But another shot rang out, and this time the bullet must've just missed. It hit my windshield and exploded in front of me.

I hadn't taken my gun out from the Jeep but another shot fired. I had no chance to get in and drive away, so I kept running through the darkness. I looked over my shoulder and saw two men coming after me.

I stopped at a tall chain-link fence and knew I'd be shot if I tried to run around. It extended far along the back parking lot of a shopping center. I jumped up and climbed over the top, threw myself on the other side and rolled when I hit the pavement.

The two men weren't far behind.

I ran along the building and another shot was fired, this time blowing out a window just over my head. I kept low and hit the end of the building, turned, and headed down a service road along Southside Boulevard.

When I looked back I could only see one man behind me, about fifty yards away. I thought four shots were fired, give or take one or two. But without knowing what kind of gun he had, he could've been down to one bullet. Or another ten.

I made my way across Southside Boulevard and into a new commercial development in the early phases of construction. I ran under a concrete structure that looked like it might eventually be a parking garage on the lower level of a building. There were thick cement columns holding up the concrete ceiling over my head. I saw a two-by-four board, grabbed it, and hid behind one of the columns. I looked the piece of wood over, and the only thought that went through my mind was I'd brought a two-by-four to a gunfight.

It was damp and dark in the concrete structure. A shadow stretched across the floor and moved toward me.

I waited behind the column and gripped the two-by-four like a baseball bat. I stuck my head out and just inches away stood the man with the gun. I stepped out and took a hard swing at the man's hand.

The gun bounced off the concrete below. And when the man bent over to pick it up, I swung the wood upward and cracked him under his chin.

I kicked the gun out of his reach and swung the two-by-four once again. This time across his back.

But he didn't go down as I'd hoped. He came at me and drove his shoulder into my chest.

I stumbled and fell back into the column, the man's arms wrapped around my waist. He lifted me up and dropped me to the ground.

On my back, I turned and spotted a long piece of rebar on the floor, stretched my arm and grabbed it. I swung it against the back of his head. I jumped to my feet and stood over him, but he swung his foot and took me back down.

I landed on top of cinder blocks. A shooting pain moved through my back and down my legs. I swore I'd broken my back the way I'd landed.

But blue lights filled the darkness from somewhere outside. Sirens whistled when a spotlight came across the man's face.

He turned and started to run but stopped and picked up his gun, then disappeared into the darkness somewhere behind the building.

Chapter 26

I SAT IN PAIN on a cold metal chair in an empty interview room at the sheriff's office's substation off Liberty Ridge Drive. I hadn't been arrested but agreed to answer any questions I could about whatever had happened after I showed up at the formerly known Dino's Pizza.

Mike Stone walked through the open door. "Can you let me get at least one night of sleep without getting yourself in trouble?" He sat down in a leather desk chair across from me, dropped a folder on the table between us. He opened it and tapped on the eight-by-ten photo on top.

I pulled the photo toward me and looked at the mug shot in front of me. "That's him."

Mike said, "Family owns that property, which led me to research the last name. Came up with a match right away. Your friend spent time down there in Raiford. Got off a murder charge but ends up getting three for drug trafficking, caught with just under two hundred grams of cocaine."

"Cocaine, huh?" I lifted the photo and looked over the next page in the folder. "This him? Conrad?"

Mike nodded. "Conrad Sokolov. Russian immigrant. Came to the US as a kid and lived with an uncle who fled the country. We've got a possible location for his whereabouts, although the source isn't very reliable. Sent a couple of officers over to check it out." He leaned back in the chair. It looked to be much more comfortable than the one I was in. "So are you going to tell me what the hell you were doing snooping around an out-of-business pizza joint in the middle of the night?"

"I was hungry," I said.

Mike heaved out a sigh of displeasure. He leaned forward on the table, his eyelids halfway over his eyes. "Would you cut the bullshit?"

I hesitated to go into it, but I knew I'd passed the point of skipping over the important details Mike could use, if he was willing to finally believe what I already knew. "This Sokolov guy delivered a pizza at the hotel, came off the elevator after Ted's body landed in the lounge chairs."

"You saw him?"

I nodded. "On camera."

"From the hotel?" He shook his head in disbelief. "We have all the footage from the hotel. We would have—"

"I guess nobody noticed the pizza being delivered by a six-foot-something man with a pizza box from a place that's out of business?"

Mike straightened out in the chair and scratched his ear. He had a dumbfounded look on his face and didn't seem to want to look me in the eye. He stood up with his hands on his hips, shaking his head. He turned and kicked the chair in front of him, sent it rolling across the room until it crashed into the white concrete wall.

He finally looked at me. "How'd you get the footage?"

I didn't think I needed to tell him the truth. "Same way I get a lot of things I need. By asking for them. You should try it sometime."

Mike kept quiet for a couple of moments, his arms now crossed over his chest. He had a pout on his face, but I knew his wheels were turning. "All right, so if this guy Conrad killed Ted Parker, then the question, of course, is why. And it doesn't sound like he was working alone." He looked down at the floor, then rubbed his face with both hands.

"I'm going to go out on a limb and say he's working for someone. Maybe a hitman for hire."

Mike narrowed his eyes and leaned with both hands down on the table between us. He pointed his long finger at my face. "Do us both a favor and keep your mouth shut. Let me think."

I laughed. "You afraid I'm going to get all the glory? You should know me enough by now. I don't want it. And no matter what, I'm happy to tell whoever you'd like that you figured it all out by yourself. You can still be the hero, Detective." I smirked at him and thought for a second he was going to reach across the table and belt me.

But he didn't. He walked away from me and pulled open the door.

"Mike," I said, before he walked out of the room.

He stopped and turned around.

I pulled out the paper I had in my pocket with the tattoo I'd drawn. "You might be able to find a connection to this. It's some kind of brotherhood or a gang of some sort. Former inmates from Raiford have them on their wrists. You'll find it on Mr. Sokolov's wrist."

Mike stared at the drawing, then stepped back to the table. He flattened it out and pulled out his phone, snapped a photo and pushed the paper back toward me. "I'll run it through a database, see what we can come up with."

"I'd bet whoever else is working with him'll have one on their wrist." He stepped out the door and without looking back, said, "You're free to go. I'll let you know if we need anything else."

I followed Mike into the hall. "That's it? You really think I'm going to go back to my boat, put my feet up?"

He shrugged. "Go get some sleep. You look like shit."

"What about Lynn Parker?" I said. "Aren't you going to get a warrant?"

Mike stopped at another office door and turned to me. "Got one already. We'll head over in the morning."

"What took so long?"

Mike gave a slight tilt to his head. "For what?"

"The warrant. Why'd you—"

"Listen, Walsh." He looked up and down the hall. "The judge wasn't too excited about this one. He didn't like the idea we were going to search a woman's house you happened to have a drink with."

"What the hell's that supposed to mean? I was poisoned, Mike. This is why I should've just gone over there myself."

"Calm your shorts, will you? We got it. It just took a little time." Mike looked me up and down. "Like I said, go get yourself some sleep. I'll let you know how it goes." He stepped into the office and started to close his door. "You know your way out."

I put my hand up and stopped the door from closing. "What if the bottle's gone by morning? What if she dumped it after I left? Too much time has passed, Mike."

He stared back at me. "I'm not going to tell you again. Go home, Walsh. I'll call you in the morning."

·· • •·• • • ··

I stopped at a 7-Eleven after I left the station. I hadn't eaten and thought I'd grab some food before I went back to my boat to try and get some rest. But the hot dogs rolling on bars behind the glass didn't look like something I wanted to eat. Neither did the cheese pizza. I grabbed a turkey sandwich wrapped in plastic from the refrigeration unit at the back. I picked up an apple, then poured myself a large black coffee.

I stepped up to the counter and pulled out my wallet to pay. When I looked through the glass toward North Julia Street, I noticed a car pulled up next to my Jeep. I paid the man behind the counter but kept my eye on the car outside. But as soon as I turned for the door, the car took off. I walked outside. I don't think I even waited for my change and watched the car turn right and disappear down Adams Street.

It was quiet, other than the ice freezer humming behind me.

I jumped into the Jeep and thought for a moment I should follow the car. But I could only assume I was being a little jumpy. Paranoid, even. After all that had happened.

· · · ● · ● ● · · ·

I sat on the edge of my bed and took off my shoes and shirt. The wounds on the back of my head caused pain when I leaned back. I stared up at the ceiling, past the point of exhaustion, and felt the dried blood in my hair.

A noise on the deck above caused me to sit up straight. I got up off the bed and tried to listen. I wondered, again, if it was paranoia. I looked at the ladder and up the hole into the darkness above.

Whatever I'd heard had stopped. But I stepped onto the first rung of the ladder and started up through the hole. I stuck my head out, and a muzzle was there waiting for me... the other end of the gun held by my Russian friend.

"I was afraid it might've been you," I said. I stepped out onto the deck with my hands up in front of me.

Conrad nodded with his chin. "You are a foolish man who seems to take a long time to learn a simple lesson. I warned you, didn't I? Yet you wouldn't listen. And your girlfriend paid the price."

I stared back at him, but I didn't respond.

"I don't know how many women you have in your life, but I hope you don't think the other one there, out in Malibu, is any safer right now."

I felt a lump in my throat. "What the hell do you want?"

"I want that formula."

My hands were still in the air. "You have the formula. It was in the briefcase."

He took a step and held the gun inches from my face. "Don't lie to me."

"So who are you working for, Conrad?"

"I don't work for anybody," he said.

"And you think I'm a liar?" I said. "That's the funniest thing I've heard all day."

He pulled back the hammer on what looked like an old Colt. "I want to know what you did with the formula."

"How many times do I have to say it? It was in the brief-case. Did you even look for it? Jesus, Conrad. It's right there under your nose, and—"

"Tell me where it is. Or you'll go from having two women in your life to none. And I'd hate to have to fly all the way out to Malibu to have to take care of your precious Annie."

"My precious Annie? I don't know where you get your information, Conrad. But she's my ex-wife. You take her out, you'd be doing me a favor."

Of course, I didn't mean that in the least. Maybe a few years back I would have, but a lot of time had gone by since our rocky, short-lived marriage had ended.

I moved my eyes around and hoped I'd spot something I could use if I got the chance. But with a gun inches from my nose, my options were limited. "I'm telling you the truth. I gave you whatever was in that briefcase."

"You have until tomorrow to get me that document. If not... Alex and Annie will pay the price." He backed away from me and stepped down onto the dock, the gun still pointed my way. "I hope you believe me. I am not lying. And if you think I am, go ahead and watch what happens."

Chapter 27

IT WAS A LITTLE before seven thirty when I pulled into Memorial. I had some time before they'd let me go inside to get Alex. It was five thirty out in Malibu, and the last thing I wanted to do was wake Annie and scare her more than I already had.

But I knew she had to be warned. I just wasn't sure what to tell her. Get out of Malibu? Go find a place to hide until I tell you it's all right to come out?

I looked at my watch and stepped out of the Jeep. I figured I'd try to talk my way in, hope someone would let me go up to Alex's room. Even if it was a little early.

· · · · · • · • · · ·

Alex sat in the chair in the corner near the window when I walked into her room.

"Must be nice to be out of bed?" I said.

"It'll be nice to get home, sleep in my own place."

The smile I tried to hold on my face dropped off. I looked back at the door and closed it. "The man who shot you... he showed up at my boat last night. Actually, just a few hours ago. I was down below trying to get a couple hours of sleep. Heard him up on the deck."

I watched her stare back at me, but I hesitated to give her all the details. "That's not what I mean. He threatened me. He said you'd be the one in danger again if I didn't hand over that formula."

Alex stared back at me without a word.

"I'll keep you safe," I said. "I promise. And we already know who he is. His name's Conrad Sokolov. Mike has a photo of him. Had me down the station to confirm the ID."

"You've seen him without the mask?"

"Yeah, last night. He showed up without one. And I think the only reason he didn't shoot me right there is he thinks I'm holding on to the formula."

There was a knock at the door. It opened and a nurse walked in. She pushed a wheelchair in front of her and smiled at Alex. "Are you ready to finally get out of here?"

Alex waved her off and pushed herself up from the chair. "I can walk. I'm fine. I feel good."

The nurse shook her head. "I'm sorry. Hospital policy. I have to take you for a ride."

Alex glanced at me and rolled her eyes. She stepped to the wheelchair, turned around, and sat down.

· · • • • • • • · ·

We pulled out of the hospital parking lot and both stayed quiet for the first couple of miles. I'd glance at Alex every couple of moments, but she just kept her eyes straight on the road.

"You okay?" I said.

She finally turned to me and smiled with a nod. "Better coming out than I was going in."

I had my eyes on the road. "Don't worry," I said. "We're going to catch this guy, and whoever else is involved. And Mike pulled a search warrant for Lynn Parker's house. I just hope it's not too late they find the bottle of Maker's Mark she poured from. If they can prove she's the one who tried to poison me, then she'll have a hard time convincing anyone else she had nothing to do with Ted's death."

Alex was quiet for a moment. "I'm sorry, Henry. But it doesn't make sense. Why would she poison you?"

"You mean, because she's the one who hired us in the first place?" I didn't have a great answer. "Maybe it's her alibi.

She hires us, and I'm right there at the hotel when this goon throws her husband off the balcony. It certainly makes her look innocent."

I could feel Alex's eyes on me.

"Is that a cut on the back of your head? I thought you said nothing happened on your boat?"

I reached back with my hand and felt the wound just above my ear. "I'll tell you all about it when we get back, if you really want to know." I shrugged. "Conrad's visit on my boat wasn't the first time I ran into him in the last twenty-four hours."

She stared back at me. "But I don't want you to worry about anything right now. Just worry about getting better, and staying safe."

I turned off University and onto Atlantic Boulevard.

"I don't have sick leave," Alex said. "So I think I need to get back to work right away. Don't you?"

"Are you serious?" I shook my head. "No way. Give me a break. You need to rest."

I could feel her watching me, but I turned into her driveway, and she smiled when she saw her neighbor—the older woman from next door—stand up from the chair on Alex's front porch.

Her dog, Raz, ran down the steps and barked when he noticed Alex. But she put her hand up and told him not to jump just as he was about to. She crouched down and wrapped her arms around him. "I missed you, Raz."

I took her bag out from the back seat and followed her and Raz up the walkway to her front door.

She hugged the woman and invited her in, but she said she had to get home.

"But let me know if you need anything," the woman said. "Anytime you need me to watch Raz, just let me know. He's the sweetest dog." She smiled. "And a good watchdog, too."

I followed Alex inside. She headed right for the couch and lay down. "I'm already tired," she said.

"It's hard to sleep in the hospital," I said. "But you've been through a lot." I walked to the window and pulled the curtain to the side. I looked down the driveway past my Jeep and into the street.

"You see something?" Alex said.

I turned to her. "No."

She got up from the couch and opened the closet door at the far end of the room. She pushed the clothes and jackets hung on a single rod to one side, and reached in. Toward the back of the closet was the gun safe she had built into the wall.

I heard a beep from the digital code on the safe. Her back was all I could see inside the closet doorway. She turned with her Glock 45 in her hand and placed it on the coffee table. She sat down on the couch and looked up at me. "You don't have to worry about me," she said. "I'll be fine."

I hesitated a moment. "This guy's legit, Alex. He's a professional, hired by whoever wanted Ted Parker dead."

"But nobody knows who he's working for," she said. "That doesn't help, unless he's caught." She picked up the Glock and rested it on her lap, her hand wrapped around the grip. "Maybe he'll make the mistake of showing up here." She looked at Raz, next to her on the couch, and ran her free hand over his head. "We're not worried, are we, Raz?"

I looked at my phone. "I wish Mike'd called by now. I would've assumed he got something from Lynn Parker's—" I stopped when I spotted something outside and turned to the window again. I pushed the curtain aside but this time saw a car pull up into the driveway. "Speak of the devil," I said. "Mike's outside."

Alex stood up and looked out the same window.

I watched her fix her hair, push a strand back behind her ear.

"He knew you were coming home today?" I said.

She didn't answer, walked past me and turned the corner toward the front door.

I heard it open, and Mike said to her, "Good to see you up and around."

Alex walked back into the room. Mike followed and gave me a nod.

"I thought you'd be at Lynn Parker's house this morning," I said.

He stood just a couple of feet into the room. His eyes went to the Glock on the coffee table, then came back to me. "There was no bottle of Maker's Mark," he said. "We got nothing."

"She must have tossed it," I said. "I told you you should've gone sooner."

Mike stepped toward me, put his finger up near my face. "I told you, Walsh, we follow procedures. We can't just fly by the seat of our pants, do whatever the hell we want. If everyone did things like you, we'd have people getting shot and killed left and right." He looked at Alex.

"Well, if you'd let me go last night, I would've found it. I guarantee it."

"Yeah, and you'd end up arrested for trespassing and B and E."

"At least I'd have what we needed," I said.

"She didn't deny you had a drink there. She said you finished the whole thing, so she put it in the recycling." He looked down at the floor. "They picked up this morning, before we got there."

"What?" I said. "Are you shitting me?" I could see on Alex's face she didn't want to get in the middle of it. "I told you, Mike. You were too late. Admit it."

I could see in his face Mike was holding something back. He was somehow calm even with me pressuring him in a way I knew he didn't like at all.

"We've got a couple officers trying to track down the truck. They'll go to the recycling center, see what they can find."

I laughed. "Yeah, I'm sure that'll be easy, find a bottle in the one place every bottle in Jax eventually ends up." I ran my hand through my hair and turned back to the window. "So now what?"

"Mrs. Parker was genuinely concerned for you, Henry. She said she was going to call you, see how you were doing, but swore up and down she had no reason to harm you."

I turned from the window. "And you believe her? Just like that?" I shook my head and again gave Alex a look. "See? This is what happens when you have to deal with all the red tape. Nothing ever gets done; people get away with murder."

"This isn't helpful," Alex said. She looked from me to Mike a few times.

"But nobody finds it odd she just happens to get rid of the bottle? And then when she turns on the charm, you just walk away: 'Oh, what a nice lady.'"

The three of us stood quiet.

"What about the other bottles?" I said.

Mike stared back at me. "What about them?"

"It seemed to me that cabana was stocked. At least from what I could tell."

"So what, then, you want us to check every bottle? Like she'd poison them all, just in case you don't drink bourbon?"

I thought for a moment. "I'm saying, what if Lynn, or someone else, poisoned all the liquor in the cabana?"

"But she was drinking herself," Alex said. "And she obviously wasn't poisoned."

I looked outside through the window. "What if the poison wasn't meant for me?"

Chapter 28

ALTHOUGH ALEX DIDN'T WANT anyone from the sheriff's office "babysitting" her, as she called it, Mike knew it was the right thing to do. He was aware Conrad Sokolov had threatened to harm Alex if I didn't come up with the so-called formula I didn't even have in my possession.

And once an officer showed up, right about the same time Alex's parents got to her house from the hotel, I slipped out and took a ride over to Lynn Parker's.

I parked the Jeep out in the street. I tossed a backpack on my shoulder and walked up the driveway, looked in the garage, but didn't see Lynn's car. The blinds on the windows were all closed.

I knocked on the front door, to be sure, and waited a couple of moments before I walked around the house to the back.

The perimeter of the yard was enclosed with a high, wrought-iron fence at least six feet tall. The vertical spires on the black fence were topped with pointed finials that extended a few inches over the top of my head. There was a chance Lynn was back by the pool, but thick, tall Japanese yew on the other side of the fence blocked my view of the backyard.

I held on to the spires and called through the fence. "Hello? Anybody back there?"

Nobody answered.

I reached up and tried to pull myself up, but these wrought-iron fences weren't meant for climbing. Just the opposite, in fact. They were almost impossible to get over. But I had no choice.

I reached up and tried to pull myself up and use my feet to push me as high as I could get. My Top-Siders actually helped me get decent traction on the wrought iron, although I'd get close to the top, and my foot would slip.

I had to use whatever strength I had to pull myself up. But I was worried about the pointed finials on top of the spires. I was aware the slightest slipup would do enough damage I'd have a tough time walking out of there.

I finally made it almost to the top and lifted my foot. With the toe of my shoe hooked on to the fence's horizontal member, I got somewhat of a bounce going and threw myself over and into the Japanese yew. I felt the pain right away, stuck between the fence and the shrub. I looked down at my leg. I'd caught it on the pointed finial, and it tore through a piece of my skin. Blood soaked through my shorts, although I was happy it was my leg and not something else.

I worked my way down toward the ground. The yew's branches tore at my skin. But then the shrub gave out, and my body crashed down to the base of the fence. My backpack was caught above me in the tree but I was able to reach for it and rip it down.

I crawled out from under and got up onto my feet. Nobody was in the yard. I peeked in through the windows on the back of the house. The curtains were open and I could see inside.

The house looked to be empty.

I walked over to the cabana and turned the knob. I expected it to be locked. But it wasn't. In fact, the door hadn't fully latched closed.

Inside, the cabana was set up somewhat like an office, with a long couch on one wall and a desk and a whiteboard on the other. There was a small wet bar on another wall and a shelf stocked with two bottles of scotch, a bottle of Canadian whiskey, two bourbons, a rye, two bottles of vodka, and a green bottle of dry vermouth. Each had been opened, the seal of each top broken. Although, the thing was, the bottles all appeared to be full.

I took my backpack off my shoulder and removed the box of mason jars I purchased at Publix on the ride over. I poured a few inches of liquor from each bottle into each individual jar, then pulled a marker from my backpack and labeled them.

I heard a noise outside and stopped what I was doing. I was almost done but had two bottles left to go. I got to my feet and looked out the crack of the cabana's door. I wasn't sure what I'd heard, but nobody was there. At least from what I could see.

I poured the vodka into the last of two jars, then from the Canadian whiskey into the final jar. I made sure the tops were twisted tight and slid all nine jars into my backpack. I peeked out through the door and made sure I was the only one in the backyard. I looked toward the house and tried to see through the windows, but I was too far away to be able to tell.

I stepped out from the cabana and walked along the shrubs and to the corner. I had a much easier time getting out of the yard than I did getting in, since all I had to do was lift the latch and swing the wrought-iron gate open.

I walked along the house and looked into the garage.

Again, the coast was clear. I walked down the driveway toward the street. But I stopped when I heard the roar of an engine.

A Porsche turned into the driveway and stopped a few feet from where I stood. The door opened, and Lynn Parker stepped out, sunglasses over her eyes.

"Henry?" she said. "What are you doing here?" She looked behind me to where my Jeep would have been if I hadn't parked down the street.

I knew right then I'd made a mistake walking down the driveway. "I was coming to talk to you," I said. "But you weren't home, so—"

"I was told you were very ill. You almost died?" She pulled her sunglasses from her eyes. "A detective and two officers came by looking for the bottle of Maker's Mark. I swear to you, I don't know how it could have happened." She squinted her eyes. "Why would I want to poison you?"

"Funny, that's the exact question I was asking myself when I realized how it happened."

"Henry, please. I—"

"What'd you do with the bottle?" I said. "Sounds to me like you were in quite the hurry to get rid of it. But I'm not gullible, like those officers who didn't seem to have a problem letting you off the hook."

She shook her head. "I told them the truth. It was recycled. What can I say? Today's the day the garbage comes. It's nothing more than pure coincidence, Henry. I know it looks suspicious, but..." She stepped back to her Porsche and reached inside. The garage door lifted open. "Go, see for yourself. The containers are empty."

I walked toward the garage and looked inside. There were two green plastic containers. Both empty.

"What makes you so certain it came from here?" she said.

I was still peering into the garage. I hesitated a moment and didn't answer her. "Then can you tell me why every bottle in that cabana is full? But the Maker's Mark just happened to be empty?" I wasn't sure there was much behind my question, but it didn't hurt to ask.

"Maker's Mark was Ted's drink. That's pretty much all he ever drank. He'd come home from work and sit by the pool, sometimes by himself, and have a glass or two to relax." She shrugged. "I'm not even sure he knew the difference between that and anything else in that cabana. But it's what he drank."

"What do you mean 'by himself?' He didn't ever drink with you? Or anyone else?"

She stared back at me for a moment before she answered. "I'd sit back there with him once in a while. But he did like to be alone. He liked to sit and think. That big brain of his was always active." She cracked a slight smile. "I think the bourbon helped him slow it down a little, so he could actually process his thoughts."

"But I mean, besides you, who else knew he kept his liquor back there in the cabana?"

She shrugged. "I don't know. It's not like he hid it or anything. Is that what you mean?"

I shook my head. "No, I mean... recently. Was anyone back there? With or without Ted? Besides you, of course?"

"Jack would come by, especially after he and Olivia split. He and Ted would have drinks once or twice a week."

"What about LJ? Or Tucker?"

She shook her head. "I don't remember the last time he was here with Ted. They were close friends, of course. But once things started to fall apart with the business..."

"And Tucker?"

"Tucker?" She paused for a moment. "I don't know."

I thought for a moment, pushed the backpack up on my shoulder. The glass jars clanked inside, and Lynn gave me a suspicious look.

"What's in your backpack?" she said.

"What? My backpack? Nothing." I started to walk past her and continued toward the street. "I'm going to get going. I'm glad we were able to talk."

"I hope you believe me, Henry. I had nothing to do with whatever happened to you." I stopped and turned but didn't respond. "I'll be in touch." I took another couple of steps.

"Why'd you park out in the street?" she said.

I stopped and turned to her. "I didn't want to block you in." I kept walking until I was out in the street, then picked up the pace, and ran the rest of the way to my Jeep.

I called Alex right away.

"Where are you now?" she said.

"I just left Lynn Parker's house."

"You what? You promised Mike you wouldn't—"

"I don't care, Alex. I wish I'd left him out of this in the first place."

"It's too late for that. And, remember, if it wasn't for Mike, I might be dead right now."

I didn't respond.

"Henry, you know he could pull your license if he wanted to. You tamper with evidence, and... "

"It's already been tampered with. Long before I got here. I still think it looks like too much of a coincidence she got rid of that bottle so fast. But she wasn't lying. Her garbage and recycling was emptied today." I thought for a moment. "I think I actually believe her."

"She's telling the truth?" Alex said.

"Like I said earlier, I'm not sure that poison was even meant for me in the first place. That bottle was Ted's. Maybe it was meant for him."

"That could make sense," she said.

"It could. And I took samples from each bottle in their cabana, where they kept some liquor. That's where Lynn poured my drink."

"You want me to make a call, see if we can get it analyzed right away?"

"I was hoping you would. It won't tell us who put something in there if we do find anything. But at least we'll know. And that would clear Lynn. In my mind, anyway."

Chapter 29

I PULLED INTO THE parking lot with the stained and faded Dino's Pizza sign in the corner near the street. The place looked even worse in the daylight, with the covered windows cracked from the outside, tall weeds shooting up from what was left of the pavement.

I drove around to the back and parked near the door. I sat and watched. I didn't know how smart it would be for me to go inside. But I couldn't imagine Conrad would still be there. He had to have been on the run at that point. At least that's what I assumed.

There were no cars anywhere. The van I'd seen the other night was still parked in the other lot.

So I took my chances and stepped out of the Jeep. The door to the back of the shuttered restaurant was cracked open.

I had protection this time. Alex had forced me to carry one of her old Smith & Wesson 9mm's after I'd left her house. I racked the slide on the pistol and lifted it out in front of me. With my foot, I pushed open the door and stepped inside.

At first it appeared to be dark inside, although once I took a few steps, a dim light shone through the open doorway.

I lowered the gun and walked to the end of the room, almost narrow, like a hallway, past chairs stacked up high against the walls on both sides. Large cardboard boxes were tipped over and paper products from inside, plates and cups and paper towels, were scattered all over the dirty linoleum floor.

I turned the corner into the kitchen area and looked toward the front of the restaurant. Sunlight slipped through the torn paper on the windows. There were pizza ovens on one side of the room and stainless steel tables on the other.

At the far end of the kitchen was a door, slightly ajar. I raised the 9mm in front of me and kicked it open.

Behind a desk sat Conrad Sokolov. His head tipped back on the headrest of the padded office chair, and his eyes were wide open, fixed on the flickering fluorescent over his head.

Dried blood had dripped from a hole in his forehead and down the front of his face. His shirt was soaked in blood.

It couldn't have been for long... but Conrad Sokolov was dead.

········

Although I called Mike Stone and told him to send the coroner, an EMS vehicle pulled into the back parking lot and parked next to my Jeep near the door.

Mike showed up a moment later, drove on two wheels into the parking lot in his Crown Victoria. Two sheriff's vehicles followed.

I stood outside the back door of the old Dino's Pizza parking lot.

Mike stepped out of his car and hurried past me through the open door. "I know you didn't kill him yourself," he said. "But if you did, I'd help you get away with it."

I followed him past the tipped boxes and paper products and through the kitchen. "How do you know I didn't do it?" I said.

He stopped outside the office door with his back to Conrad's body, looked behind him, then turned back to me, pointed to his forehead. "I don't believe you're a good enough shot to hit him dead center like that. Even standing from here." He snorted out a slight laugh and shook his head. He reached inside his jacket and pulled out a cigarette.

He stuck it in his mouth but let it hang from his lips without lighting it. With a nod, he said, "You don't even carry, do you?"

I pulled my shirt down tight to cover the Smith & Wesson tucked into the waist of my pants. "No, not usually."

He looked back toward the body and the EMS techs inside the office. He turned back to me. "So are you going to tell me why you came here? Looks to me you already broke your promise. I thought you agreed to stay out of the way."

"Did I?" I said. But didn't answer his question.

Mike stood just outside the office with his back to Conrad and the EMS techs. He pulled a lighter from his pocket and lit the cigarette in his mouth.

The two EMS technicians stepped out from the office and walked past me and Mike. "All yours," one of them said.

I stood in the doorway and watched Mike stand over Conrad's body. He got his face close, stared at the bullet wound in Conrad's head.

"Did you know the owner of this place disappeared?" I said.

Without looking back at me, Mike nodded. "What do you think we do all day, wait for you to give us the breaking news?" He gave me a quick glance from the corner of his eye.

"I'm glad to see you at least do some research, not just start fights, hoping someone will spill the beans."

I'd gotten used to Mike's attitude and constant digs. I knew it made him feel like he had the upper hand. Like a bully in the schoolyard.

Mike nodded toward the body. "He was this one's uncle. Suspect he might've gotten in some trouble over here, probably went back to Russia. Family never heard from him again."

"What about the time he spent in prison? Did that have anything to do with the uncle?" I said.

Mike straightened up from studying the body and walked out of the office. He stopped and looked around the kitchen, his eyes squinted. "Separate, as far as I know. Should've gone down for murder, but somehow he got away with it. Maybe if someone had done their job, he'd still be behind bars."

I was surprised to hear Mike question anybody's work at the sheriff's office. But the tone of his voice told me he was more annoyed than usual, and perhaps there was more about Conrad than he was letting on.

Three officers and another plainclothes officer walked past us toward the office with Conrad's body.

Mike walked out to the front of the restaurant. There were a couple of tables without chairs but otherwise nothing much to see. He kept quiet, walked past me again and straight through the back and out the door.

I got the feeling he was trying hard to get away from me.

He walked to his car and pulled open the driver's side door.

"Any luck on finding that bottle?" I said, although not about to let him know I'd gone back to Lynn Parker's house.

He put one foot inside and turned to me. He pulled sunglasses from inside his jacket, slipped them over his eyes and shook his head. "She didn't poison you, Walsh."

I hesitated a moment. "You're right," I said. Words you'd rarely hear me say out loud to Mike unless I really had to.

Mike had started to duck into his car but stopped and cocked his head. "I'm right?" He nodded. "Good to know we're on the same page."

"But someone poisoned that bottle. It's just that it wasn't meant for me."

Mike had his eyes out toward the street as the EMS vehicle pulled away.

I said, "One of his business partners can tell us who it was."

Mike shook his head. "I don't think so. They're clean." He ducked back into the driver's seat and tried to pull his door closed, but I grabbed it with my hand.

"Move your goddamn hands, Walsh."

"You expect one of 'em to come right out, tell you he's a criminal?" I said.

Mike yanked the car door closed, started the engine, and took off out of the parking lot.

Chapter 30

I LOOKED DOWN INTO my glass of Jack Daniels and rolled around the two cubes of ice inside.

"Are you ever going to use your office upstairs again?" Billy said. "You're hardly ever up there."

I sipped my Jack and nodded. "Maybe once things get back to normal, whenever that'll be."

"You mean when Alex is back on her feet?"

I thought for a moment. "I'll be honest," I said, "I don't know what her plans are going forward. She's been shot twice in under a year. I don't think it's exactly what she signed up for."

Billy shook his head. "You're not giving her much credit. It takes a lot more than a couple of gunshots to take her down. The only thing that'll stop her is—"

"Death?" I said before he could even finish. "Because she was pretty damn close this time."

Billy removed a glass from the dishwasher in front of him and wiped it out with a towel, hung the glass on the rack above his head. "She won't quit," he said. "Not until you tell her to."

I laughed. "You think she'd listen to me?"

"No more than you'd listen to her if she told you to quit." Billy leaned on the bar with both hands. "And I think she'd be afraid of letting you down."

"Bullshit," I said. "I'm the last person who'd—"

"She'd step in front of a moving train for you," Billy said. He grabbed another glass from the dishwasher, wiped out the inside and hung it up on the rack.

Before I could say another word he turned and walked to the other side of the bar where a young couple had just sat down.

I finished what was left in my glass and got up from my stool. "Be right back," I said loud enough for Billy to hear.

He turned and gave a thumbs-up, and I walked out the door to call Alex. I stood in the back parking lot, my eyes out on the St. Johns. I thought about all we'd been through, both me and Alex, and wondered how much longer we could keep it up.

I dialed, and the phone rang three or four times before Alex answered.

"Hey," she said. "Where are you?"

I looked up at the second floor above the restaurant. "At the office," I said. "Actually, outside the office. I'm standing in the parking lot getting some fresh air. I was going to come over but knew Mike was going to be there."

"He just left," she said. "I think he thought I'd be happy Sokolov was dead."

"You're not?" I said.

"We needed him alive."

I thought for a moment. "You're right. But I'm afraid Mike'd like to think he worked alone. But I don't believe it. Not for a second."

"I'm not sure that's what he believes," Alex said.

"No?"

"Don't you know him by now? He listens to you, Henry. He has so much respect for you. He just has his own way of showing it."

"You mean, by not showing it? Because that's the way I see it. Sometimes I think that means proving me wrong, so he can get all the glory himself."

"But you don't," she said. "So what'd it matter? Let him get the glory."

I walked across the lot, the phone up against my ear. "I was thinking," I said. "I'd like to look into the security staff at

Chemcore... see who they are... where they came from. And maybe who's behind the hiring."

"Of the security staff?"

"Yes."

"You want me to look into it?"

"Are you up for it?" I said.

"Of course. I told you I am."

"And you're feeling okay?"

She paused a moment before she answered. "I'm not sure I'm ready to chase someone on foot. But I can look into it, if that's what you're asking?"

"Only if you're up for it," I said.

"Henry, come on. If there's something I can't do, you'll be the first to know."

· · · · ●●● · · · ·

Jack Parker came right to his door when I knocked from outside in the hall. "Henry?" he said, a drink in one hand. The inside of his apartment looked dark, other than light from a TV. He looked at his watch. "I wasn't expecting you to—"

"The man who killed Alex is dead," I said. "And right now, it looks like he's the same man who, uh, sent your brother off that balcony."

"What? You found him? I mean... Are you sure?"

"That he's the same man who killed Ted?" I shook my head. "No, I'm not. And I'm not a betting man, but if I had to bet... "

"Who?" he said, his eyes wide open like I'd more than just caught him off guard with what I'd just told him.

"His name's Conrad Sokolov."

"Conrad Sokolov? Who exactly is he? I mean, why would this man—"

"So you've never heard the name?" I said, before he could finish asking a question I still didn't have an answer for. "Did Ted ever mention anything to you about Russians who might've been involved in his business in one way or another?"

Jack laughed, although it wasn't filled with joy. "Russians? Heavens, I can't imagine so. Are you telling me you think Ted was involved in some kind of international crime, like some goddamn espionage movie?"

I stared back at him through the doorway but didn't respond. "So you've never heard that name before?"

Jack shook his head. "No. Never."

I waited a moment, unsure if he was going to give me something more. But he appeared as surprised as anyone might be to hear his brother may have been murdered by some Russian thug.

"I don't think this guy's any kind of a ringleader. Maybe the head thug. But someone hired him to kill Ted. And anyone who got in his way."

Jack turned and looked over his shoulder into his apartment. The way he stood—one hand up on the doorframe—seemed like he didn't want to welcome me into his apartment. Whether or not he had something to hide on the other side of the door, I didn't know.

"You killed him?" Jack said.

"No. The last thing we needed was this guy to end up dead."

"So, then, who shot him?"

I went through the last few moments of our conversation and tried to remember exactly what details I'd given him. "I'd guess whoever wanted to keep him quiet," I said. "He was close to being caught."

Jack looked down at the floor.

"Something you want to tell me, Jack?"

He looked up and shook his head. "Me? No. I... How will you find out who hired him?"

I took a moment before I answered. "I can't answer that right now. But don't worry. When I figure it out, you'll be the first to know."

Chapter 31

LJ Hoover sat in his black BMW on Memorial Park Drive, his head down and his phone in his lap. He seemed startled when I knocked on his window. He pushed open the door and stepped out but kept his eyes on his phone and tapped on it with his thumbs. "Sorry, just finishing a message." He looked up at me and slipped the phone in his pocket. "How's your partner?"

"Alex? She's doing all right so far."

LJ slowly nodded. "That's good news, right?"

I didn't respond. "I'm not here for small talk," I said. "What do you know about Conrad Sokolov?"

LJ held his gaze on me for a moment. "Conrad who?"

"Conrad Sokolov. He's the man who we believe shot Alex. And probably responsible for Ted's death. But he's come after me, looking for that formula." I leaned with one hand down on the front fender of LJ's BMW.

His eyes shifted to where I'd placed my hand.

"Do you mind moving your hand?" he said. "I just had it waxed."

I stepped away from his car. "Sorry, I don't know what it's like to own a car you're afraid to touch." I crossed my arms. "So, this guy Conrad... seems to've escaped a murder charge, but spent three years in Raiford for trafficking cocaine."

LJ looked away, and watched the cars driving by on the street.

"Was Ted into the powder, by any chance?" I said.

LJ's eyebrows shot up. "Ted? Cocaine? Nah, no way. Ted was straight as they come."

"What about you?" I said.

LJ pointed to himself, the tip of his finger poked into his chest. "Me?" He stared back at me and shook his head but didn't really answer.

"Well, it's just... we've got this dead guy who seems to've been a drug dealer but also a hitman or thug of some sort. He was at the hotel the night of Ted's death. And I think we both know someone who"—I touched the side of my nose—"liked the nose candy every now and then."

"Olivia?" LJ said. "Honestly, I knew nothing about that."

"Are you going to try to tell me you and Olivia didn't have some kind of relationship that maybe wasn't all business?"

LJ started to move his mouth but stopped before words came out.

"Olivia's neighbor happened to mention a BMW he'd noticed in her driveway that didn't belong to her. And Conrad drove a Cadillac. The neighbor said he'd see it there at all hours."

"You think I'm the only person Olivia knows with a BMW?" he said.

I laughed. "Good one." I leaned with my hand back down on the front left fender. "All right, LJ. It's time to come clean and tell me the truth." I looked him in the eye. "Were you sleeping with Olivia? Is that why you were at the hotel?"

"No, I was not sleeping with Olivia. I mean, we got along well. But it really was strictly business between us. That's the truth."

"Your wife doesn't seem to believe that," I said.

LJ let out a deep sigh. "What do you want me to tell you? It's not like I can prove it."

"No, you can't," I said. "But you can start with the fact you and Olivia were at the hotel together. And then Ted hits the pavement out back. Olivia snorts a line of coke laced with fentanyl. So now it just so happens you're the last man standing. You want to tell me that's just a coincidence? Or dumb luck?"

"If you're trying to accuse me of—"

"I just want the truth, LJ. Lying to me about it doesn't do anything. And your wife'll need some convincing herself."

"Vanessa has always believed I was cheating on her. But I never have. Now she's got it in her mind that me and Olivia were sleeping together. But she's wrong." He pulled a kerchief from his pocket and used it to wipe the back of his neck. He looked down at the sidewalk. "I love my wife, you know. But she's a jealous person. Paranoid, even." He raised his eyes to mine. "And I have no idea who this Conrad Sokolov guy is. It sounds like maybe Olivia did, if he's who sold her that cocaine."

"Then why don't you tell me what your meeting was about?"

"At the hotel?"

"Yes, the afternoon before Ted was killed."

LJ paused. "Ted was the one who set it up. He asked us to meet him there. Olivia, too."

"About what? The three of you sit around getting wasted in the hotel room?"

"No!" LJ snapped. "Wasn't my game. I told you that. And Ted... I wouldn't say he was straight or anything, but he didn't do drugs. Not that I'm aware of. He liked his booze. Drank Maker's Mark. That was his thing."

"So if you weren't there to sleep with Olivia, and you weren't there to party, then what was this so-called meeting all about?"

LJ looked back into his car. "Ted wanted me to come back into the business. But I told him I couldn't handle the secrets. The goddamn formula. If he couldn't trust his best friend, then I didn't see how it could work. He told me Olivia had it locked up at her house."

"The briefcase?" I said. "There was money inside it. And a couple of guns."

"I don't know anything about money... or guns." He put up his hands. "Not my thing."

I looked at his Beemer. "Money's not your thing?"

He cracked a slight smile. "Guns."

I wasn't sure I believed him.

"Ted didn't trust Tucker. He knew he couldn't trust him and knew Tucker would need the original formula to maximize profits if he could persuade Ted to sell. So Ted and I would meet, even after I'd left Chemcore, and discuss how to get Tucker out of there."

"But why meet at the hotel when you both live in Jax. I don't get that. There are dozens of places all over Florida. Like coffee shops and... "

"Olivia didn't have an office and spent a lot of her time on the road. Even if it wasn't that far of a drive for her, she'd have a few drinks..." He let out a slight laugh. "She could drink anyone under the table. But then she'd use her credit card miles, stay at whatever hotel she was at for free instead of getting behind the wheel."

"So if you had already left, then why was Olivia still there later that evening?"

"Maybe she was with Ted?" he said.

"With Ted? You mean—"

"Oh no, I don't mean together like that. That would never happen." He shrugged. "I guess I can't answer why he stayed that night. Maybe he just didn't want to go home to Lynn. Their marriage had been on the rocks for some time, although for some reason they stayed together."

Chapter 32

I WALKED UP THE backstairs to my office, surprised to see a dim light turned on inside. I was the last person to ever leave a light on and knew I'd turned it off. Of course, Conrad was dead. But I wasn't about to take any chances. So I pulled the Smith & Wesson from my pants and reached for the knob. I turned it, slowly, to see if it was unlocked.

And it was.

I raised the gun and pushed open the door.

What sounded like a vicious bark scared the hell out of me. I was glad I didn't pull the trigger because Alex's dog, Raz, charged at me and stuck his nose in my crotch.

I patted him on the head and turned to Alex, seated on the couch with her feet up, the laptop open in front of her.

She eyeballed the gun in my hand. "What the hell are you doing with that? Don't you think I've been shot enough?"

I walked to my desk and placed the Smith & Wesson on top. "What are you doing here?" I said.

She sat up straight on the couch.

"Oh, I'm sorry. I thought you'd be happy to see me."

I plopped down next to her and leaned my head back on the cushion behind me. "Aren't you supposed to be home, resting?"

"I've rested enough," she said, a big smile on her face. "I feel pretty good." She turned her computer screen toward me. "I just got the results from the lab. They were all clean."

"Clean? There was nothing?"

She shook her head. It doesn't mean she didn't try to poison you."

"Actually," I said. "I don't think she did."

"Why not?"

I took a moment before I answered. "Because it makes no sense."

"Do you think she tried to poison Ted? And maybe failed?"

I rubbed my tired face up and down. "Right now, we have no motive. And I can't come up with a single reason why she'd hire us to see if Ted was having an affair if her real goal was to have him killed, or do it herself."

Alex sat quiet, closed the lid on her laptop and placed it down next to her.

I got up from the couch and looked out the window at the St. Johns. "I met with LJ over at Memorial Park... before I came back here. Turns out, if he's telling the truth, the three of them met to discuss LJ going back to Chemcore. From what LJ said, Ted wanted to get Tucker out of the business."

"So if Tucker got wind of what Ted was up to... "

"He wouldn't be happy, to put it lightly."

Alex got up and put a mug of water in the microwave. She waited with her back to me without saying a word. The bell dinged and she turned with her mug. Steam poured off the top, and she dropped a tea bag inside. She walked back to the couch and sat down. "Something doesn't make sense," she said. "What happened to Olivia's company wanting to buy Chemcore? Wasn't that the original story?"

"From what I was told," I said. "But it doesn't mean Olivia was all for it though. Maybe she was more interested in helping Ted keep control. Or if Tucker was the one pushing for a sale, it'd make sense Ted would do whatever he could to stop it."

· · · · •·•· · · ·

I left Alex at the office and took a ride out to Westside Industrial Park where Chemcore's offices were located. I parked in front of the Chemcore Incorporated sign and walked into the lobby of the building. A security guard I didn't recall seeing before sat in a bar-height chair. He didn't have much of a neck, and his fat hung over the edge of the stool. He stared back at me without a word.

"I'm here to see Tucker Dennison," I said.

He didn't answer right away as if to set the tone that he was the authority in the room and wasn't going to be pushed around. He sniffled his nose and shook his head. "Not here today."

"No?" I turned and looked out the glass door into the parking lot. "Isn't that his car out there?"

The man stood from his seat, and towered over my six-two frame. He held his gaze on me for a moment, his eyes narrowed. He looked toward the parking lot and nodded. "Yup, that's his car. But like I said... he's not here." He folded his arms and rested them on the mound of a stomach over his belt.

"Can you just tell him Henry Walsh is here?"

The man dropped his trunk-like arms by his side and eased up from the stool. His skin was covered in tattoos. I looked for a match to the one I saw on the back of Conrad's wrist but didn't see anything other than some dragons and crosses running up and down his arms.

He turned and opened a door behind him, walked through, and closed it shut.

But a moment later the door opened again. Another uniformed man walked out behind the other. I recognized him from the first time I'd stopped to visit Tucker.

"Mr. Walsh?" said the man.

"That's me."

He looked me up and down. "Come with me."

I followed the man through the doorway and down a long hall until we got to an elevator.

The man didn't say a word, and I stayed quiet, assuming I'd have another face-to-face with Tucker Dennison.

We stepped on the elevator when the door opened and took it down below ground level.

"I'm not here alone," I said. "So if you're planning to do something I'm not going to like, just keep that in mind. They'll be here in no time."

The man turned and glanced at me, then gestured for me to walk ahead of him when the door once again opened.

A strong, burning chemical smell filled the air.

I followed the security guard down the hall and stopped.

Tucker stepped in front of me and wore a white lab coat. He nodded to his friend. "Thank you, I'll take it from here."

The security guard nodded, then turned and walked down the hall and stepped back onto the elevator.

Tucker turned and walked ahead of me down the hall. "Follow me," he said.

We walked past windowed laboratories and conference rooms. The light overhead was as bright as sunlight and reflected off the white walls. The only sounds down there were of doors opening and closing. Voices could be heard from the other side of the walls.

"I've been expecting you," he said, still at a pace a few steps ahead of me. He stopped at a large steel door and put his palm up on a black pad-like device on the wall. A red light flashed and something beeped. Tucker pushed open the door.

I followed him inside the room, white and sterile like the hallway. A long glass table took up most of the space, surrounded by at least a dozen black office chairs.

Tucker sat on the far end of the table and gestured toward the chairs. "Please, have a seat."

I looked around, unsure where I was or what was about to happen. After a brief moment, I sat and removed the 9mm in my waistband. I placed it up on the table.

"I don't think you'll need that," he said. He held his gaze on me for a moment. "I must admit, you're very persistent, although I'm not exactly sure what you're even after at this point."

I narrowed my eyes. "I want the truth," I said. "And nobody seems to know what that is around here. I want the truth about what happened to Ted. I want to know about you and LJ and what the hell the story is with this goddamn formula everyone's after."

Tucker leaned forward on the table. "Maybe I can clear some things up for you," he said.

"How about you start by admitting you didn't like Ted destroying your chance to cash in on millions of dollars because he refused to sell the company."

Tucker stared at me without a word, like he was holding back a smile. "I can tell you the truth you're after."

"And what makes you think I'll believe a word coming out of your mouth?"

Tucker held his hands out, his palms toward me. "Give me a chance to explain." He got up from the table and turned to the wall. He tapped a panel of buttons, and the entire wall shifted and slid open like an elevator door. Tucker reached inside the opening and turned around with a notebook in his hands. He tossed it down in front of me on the table. "Go ahead. Take a look."

I opened the notebook and flipped through the pages. What I saw, as far as I could tell, looked exactly like what I'd found in the briefcase inside the trunk of the Cadillac. "Where'd you get this?" I said.

Tucker nodded toward the hidden opening inside the wall. "It's been kept inside this wall since we started Chemcore."

"But this is what was inside the briefcase. My partner was shot because of this."

Tucker shook his head. "What Ted took to that hotel room was a fake," he said.

"You set him up?"

"Did I set him up?" Tucker shook his head. "I wouldn't do that to Ted."

I stared at the numbers and figures in the notebook. "I don't understand. I thought Ted gave it to Olivia and LJ to keep it from you?"

"Is that what you heard?" he said. "Let me guess. LJ told you that?"

I didn't answer. "Are you going to try and tell me you're the only one who's not lying? That you were Ted's real friend? Because everybody claims to be his friend, but I'm not exactly sure if anyone was."

Tucker sat down in the chair at the end of the table. "You said you wanted the truth. I'm trying to give it to you if you'd give me a chance."

I leaned forward and pointed my finger at Tucker's face. "Then tell me what the hell's going on."

"LJ wanted revenge."

"Revenge? For what? Because you forced him out?"

"Not at all. In fact, Ted and I were on the same team. LJ was the one who was going to destroy this company. Everything we built here. All LJ wanted was the glory. And the money."

"That's funny," I said. "It's my understanding you were the one after the money. Ted and LJ were the ones who—"

"I'll give LJ credit. He can weave quite a tale. He's always been quite the storyteller. Which I guess made him the ideal salesman. If anyone could sell ice to Eskimos, it was LJ."

I still couldn't wrap my head around what was going on. And I had no way of knowing if Tucker was telling the truth or not. I picked up the notebook. "So this is the same one I showed you outside your tennis club?"

He shook his head. "You never gave it to me, did you?"

"No, but… "

"Well, then, there's your answer. I'm telling you, Mr. Walsh, the real formula hasn't left this building. It hasn't left this room. We wanted LJ to have it. I don't mean this one... the, uh, fake one. Ted wrote up all those formulas just to throw LJ off. I mean, it took some convincing. Ted didn't want to believe LJ would turn on him like he did. So that night in the hotel... he set him up. Olivia was there to help him do it."

"And it cost her her life," I said.

Tucker looked down at his hands on the table. "I had no idea LJ would take everything to the extreme."

"By taking it to the extreme, you mean having anyone killed who got in his way?"

Tucker shook his head. "I don't believe LJ killed Ted."

Chapter 33

Lynn Parker stood outside her front door when I stepped from the Jeep parked in her driveway. She didn't move or invite me inside when I walked toward her.

"Are you going to try to blame me for anything else?" she said.

"No," I said. "I'm here to apologize."

"You honestly believed I would have poisoned you, Henry? I just wanted you to have a drink with me. There was nothing more to it."

"I know," I said. "But the reason I want to say I'm sorry is because I didn't give you the information you hired me to find."

Lynn shrugged. "Well, I don't think either of us ever expected Ted would have—"

"I'm afraid you were right," I said. "You were right from the beginning... about Ted. Because he was having an affair."

Lynn had a blank stare on her face, clearly caught off guard by what I'd said. She turned and opened her front door. "Maybe we should go inside."

I followed her down the hall and into the living room, with the TV on the wall and two leather couches facing each other.

"Please, have a seat," she said. "Can I get you a drink?"

I didn't find it funny, but I let out a slight laugh. "No, I think I'll hold off for now."

Lynn looked like she took a moment to understand what I meant. "Oh, right."

We sat down across from each other; a square maple-colored coffee table between us.

"You never mentioned a word about Olivia to me, so I'm going to assume you never once suspected there could have been something between them?" I said.

Lynn's eyes opened wide. "Ted and Olivia?" She shook her head, placed her hand flat over her chest. "Those two were like brother and sister."

I looked up at whatever was playing on the TV. The volume was turned off. "They were sleeping together," I said.

Lynn busted out a short, ear-piercing squeal of a laugh. "Ted and Olivia?" She shook her head. "Not a chance in hell that would ever happen. If you knew the things Ted used to say about her, back when she was married to Jack." She kept the smile on her face, but it started to fade as she gazed back at the stone-cold look on mine.

"I'm sorry," I said after a brief pause. "But it appears to be true, from what I've learned. Ted and Olivia were having an affair."

Lynn stared back at me. She opened her mouth to speak but stopped. She swallowed hard. "It... it can't be true. I don't believe it. And Ted... Ted would never do that to his brother."

I sat, quiet. "I'm sorry."

With a slight tilt to her head, she said, "You're serious? But... but if Jack ever found out, he'd... " She didn't finish her thought. She didn't have to.

"Do you know the last time Jack was here?" I said.

She took a moment before she finally shook her head. "No, I don't. I don't know. Why?"

"Can you just try and remember the last time you saw him? Maybe out back? Having a drink with Ted?"

Lynn sat back on the couch and stared straight ahead. She turned to the window and looked out toward the yard out back. "He was here a couple days before Ted's death."

"Was he here with Ted?"

She had a blank look in her eyes. She took a moment before she answered. "No. He came during the day, when Ted was at work."

"For what? To see you?" I said.

"He sat right there on the couch, where you're sitting. I remember thinking he'd acted strange. Fidgety. I mean, he was always a little odd but... " She put her hand over her mouth, her eyes wide open. "Jack was outside. He went out back by the pool. He told me he had to make a business call. He went outside so he could have some privacy." She stared back at me. Her breathing sounded erratic, like she had trouble catching her breath.

"Did you see him go in that cabana at any point?" I said.

After a moment, she nodded. "Do you think Jack... " She stopped and got up from the couch. She paced in front of the window, her eyes toward the floor. She stopped and turned to the window.

"Lynn?"

She had tears in her eyes.

"Can you call him?" I said.

Lynn rubbed her face with both hands and wiped away her tears. "What am I supposed to say? Ask him if he tried to poison Ted?"

"No," I said. "Tell him you know what happened to Ted. But don't mention anything else. Don't mention my name."

"What? But what if he—"

"Don't say anything else," I said. "Just leave it at that." I got up from the couch. "Just give me about twenty minutes before you call him. I'll be back."

· · · · •· •· • · ·

My phone rang when I backed out of Olivia's neighbor's house. I knew who it was before I answered.

"Hi, Jack," I said.

"Henry? What the hell's going on?"

Of course, I acted surprised. "Going on with what?"

Lynn just called me. She said she knows what happened to Ted. She was hysterical, crying into the phone, and—"

"Where are you?" I said.

"I'm going over to her house, see what this is all about."

"Oh, good."

"Good? Why? What do you know about this, Henry? What the hell's she talking about?"

"You sure you don't know what she's talking about?" I said.

I heard a click and looked at my phone's screen.

Jack had hung up.

· · • • • • • • · ·

Lynn's car was out in the driveway and Jack was parked right behind it.

I had parked the Jeep out on the street and walked up to Lynn's front door. I knocked but she didn't answer. I turned and looked back toward the street when I heard Mike Stone's Crown Victoria pull in the driveway behind me.

Another sheriff's vehicle pulled in behind him, pulled over, and parked on the grass.

The door still hadn't opened, so I knocked again and pulled out my phone at the same time. I dialed Lynn's number.

Jack answered her phone. "What the hell do you think you're doing?" he said.

"How about you open the door, and let me in and we can talk," I said.

"How about you tell those officers who just walked around back of this house to get lost first. Then maybe I'll let you inside."

I covered the mic on the phone with my hand and turned back to Mike. "Can't they hold up back there?" I said.

Mike gave me a nod and walked around the corner after the officers.

"I'm serious, Henry," Jack said. "Those officers come inside this yard, Lynn's blood'll be on your hands."

"Jack, don't," I said. "Just listen to me. Open the door, okay?"

I heard his heavy breathing through the phone.

A moment later the front door opened. Jack stood behind the glass storm door and had Lynn in front of him. The muzzle of his gun was inches from her face. He pushed open the door and pulled her down the steps, his arm wrapped around her neck.

"Let her go," I said.

Jack laughed. "I gotta give you credit. I don't know how you did it. But I give you credit. Better than the sheriff's office could ever do, right?"

Mike Stone walked around from the back of the house. He had his gun drawn and pointed toward Jack. "Drop the gun," he said.

Jack shook his head. "How about this?" He gave me a nod with his chin. "Why don't you let me and Henry talk." He turned to Mike and the two officers. "You three can get in your cars and get lost."

"Jack, it's over," I said. "There's no way you'll—"

"Over?" he yelled. "It'll be over for Lynn if the three little pigs don't get out of here." Jack's face was a bit twisted, his eyebrows tight over his eyes.

"I'm not going anywhere," Mike said. He kept his gun on Jack.

Jack rolled his eyes. He looked at me and nodded his head to the side toward Mike. "This guy's the hero, right? The shooter up on the roof?"

I looked at Mike and knew he wasn't going anywhere.

"Jack, just let her go," I said. "Time to give up."

He shook his head. "How the hell'd you figure it out?" he said. "I guess I made a mistake and underestimated you. A guy drinks as much as you do... "

"I can handle my booze pretty well," I said. "Unless I accidentally drink the poison someone left for his brother."

Jack had a smirk on his face.

"You knew all about Ted and Olivia all along," I said. "And when you met Conrad, you thought you had the perfect plan. You even knew Olivia wouldn't be able to resist a good line of coke after all those years."

"Once a cokehead, always a cokehead," he said.

"But you couldn't afford Conrad, so you told him about Ted's formula. You knew it was worth millions to the right people. But you and Conrad were too stupid to know it wasn't even the right one. Those formulas in that notebook you took from Olivia weren't worth the paper they were written on."

"How do you know it was fake?"

I stared back at him but didn't answer. Ted told you about the setup to see if LJ would turn around and sell it. But he was smart enough to know he couldn't trust you enough to tell you it wasn't the real thing. But it was too late once you figured it out."

Lynn tried to wrestle herself away from Jack. "Please, just let me go!" Her voice cracked.

Jack pulled her tighter, her neck inside the bend of his arm.

Mike took another step closer to Jack. "Let her go!" he snapped. "I'm telling you right now." He took a quick glance at me from the corner of his eye. "I find it hard to believe this is all because his brother and his ex-wife slept together?"

"He was sleeping with her long before she left me," Jack snapped. "My brother knew how to keep a secret, that's for sure."

"I'm going to pull this trigger if you don't let her go," Mike said.

The two officers came up around the other side of the house, both with their guns drawn.

"Jack, there's no good way out of this," I said. I looked at Mike and hoped he wasn't going to take a chance and pull that trigger. "So what about Conrad?" I said to Jack. "Why'd you kill him?"

"He was sloppy."

"You mean... after he got Olivia to snort the cocaine laced with fentanyl?" I said.

Jack started to step back toward the door. He dragged Lynn along with him, then switched the gun into his other hand and kept his arm around her neck from behind. He reached back to open the door with his free hand and kept his eyes on me and Mike. "Don't do anything stupid," Jack said. "Or she's dead."

"Jack, please," Lynn cried. "I didn't do anything!"

Jack took another step back into the open doorway.

A gun appeared behind him from the darkness inside the house and was pointed at the back of his head.

"Drop the gun."

Alex stepped out from behind the wall, her Glock pressed up against his skull.

Mike rushed forward, held his gun on Jack, and pulled Lynn away from him with his free hand. "There's nowhere to go," he said to Jack.

Lynn slid down to the ground and crawled down the steps and away from Jack.

Jack spun around, took a wild swing at Alex with the gun still in his hand.

But she ducked low and came up with a punch and caught him where a man never wants to be hit.

Jack's eyes rolled back, and Mike tackled him to the ground.

The two officers jumped forward and helped Mike to his feet, pinned Jack down, and slapped the cuffs on him, and one officer read him his rights.

Sirens screamed in the distance and grew louder as they drove closer.

The officers lifted Jack to his feet, dragged him away, and threw him in the back of the sheriff's vehicle.

Lynn got up off the ground, threw herself into my arms and cried. I held her and looked back at Alex and smiled. "It's good to have you back on your feet," I said.

· · · · · · · · · ·

Thank you for reading *Dropped Dead*. If you enjoyed the story, please leave a review wherever you purchased it. If you're ready for more, the adventure continues with the next book in the series, *Dead Luck*. Find out more by visiting: GregoryPayette.com

Sign up for the newsletter on my website:

GregoryPayette.com

Once or twice a month I'll send you updates and news. Plus, you'll be the first to hear about new releases with special prices. If you'd like to receive the Henry Walsh prequel (for free) use the sign-up form here:

GregoryPayette.com/crossroad

Also by Gregory Payette

Visit GregoryPayette.com for the complete catalog:

HENRY WALSH MYSTERIES

Dead at Third

The Last Ride

The Crystal Pelican

The Night the Music Died

Dead Men Don't Smile

Dead in the Creek

Dropped Dead

Dead Luck

A Shot in the Dark

JOE SHELDON SERIES

Play It Cool

Play It Again

Play It Down

U.S. MARSHAL CHARLIE HARLOW

Shake the Trees

Trackdown

JAKE HORN MYSTERIES

Murder at Morrissey Motel

STANDALONES

Biscayne Boogie

Tell Them I'm Dead

GREGORY PAYETTE

Drag the Man Down
Half Cocked
Danny Womack's .38